To Mandy

I only met you for a few days but it was a great experience.
Believe it or not your views after that had a very positive effect
I will always be forever grateful you introduced me to Sligo's west coast - a place I intend to visit many more times.
You will always be a special person to me Mandy.

Phil

XXX

Copyright Notice

Chapter One

WE had two meetings a day. One at the start, telling us we had to sell lots and lots and how much business we needed to write to achieve our monthly and team targets. It was all there in front of us on the whiteboard. The board of shame. We returned to the meeting room at the end of the day. The purpose of this was so our sales manager could send us home feeling bad, inspiring us to jump off the first available bridge or beat ourselves with sticks, proving he was right, and we were not worthy. It had become clear to me at the start of the third week I would not hit this month's target. During each of Dave Ballinger's twice daily meetings, not only did he make it clear we were useless, but he also reminded us that two consecutive poor months would lead to a trip to the Job Centre. My future was clear, after under target figures last month, I would be seeking employment elsewhere leaving without a thank you, or even an acknowledgement that I still existed.

The only good thing that happened to me during my workday in Birmingham was walking out of the revolving door at Saturn House, where the offices of White Beam were located on the third floor. I now had a whole weekend to forget about targets and losing my job. The offer of a drink with Danny Blanch was tempting, but I knew I would not be able to down just a couple of pints of the black stuff after my day in the office.

Joining Danny, would have resulted in drinking until my legs refused to react with the rest of my body. I was skint and did not have the £30 or £40 to spend on beer. Both my cards were at the limit. If I used all my overdraft and lived without eating, I might just make it to payday in a week's time. Since me and Angie split up about six months ago, I spent the minimum on food. Just a couple of nights out per month were all I had to look forward to. No life for a 29-year-old and the future looked even more bleak.

Chapter Two

I trudged across the city centre with myriads of workers rushing for buses and trains to sit down for diner with their partners or like me cooking an express meal to eat in front of the TV before sleeping alone and doing it all again tomorrow. I was depressed. Down, but not quite out. The stocky Big Issue seller at the entrance to the small railway station gave me a nod. As usual, I gave him a pound. Nowhere near the cover price of the magazine, but I could never afford to buy a copy. Still, I felt I was doing my bit for a man trying to get his life back on track. Time to join the rush through the corridor and down the elevator - just three minutes to wait on the platform. The train had filled up at Moor Street station at the other side of the city centre and like most evenings I had to stand shoulder to shoulder in cramped conditions, my ribs regularly knocked and accompanied by the unavoidable waft of body odour until passengers got off at Rowley Regis. I stood close to an attractive blonde woman with short peroxide hair. We had been smiling at each other for three days and I had failed to conjure up the courage to speak to her. Today was no different. I thought to myself, what's the point, I can't afford to take her out anyway. The petite smartly dressed commuter in her mid-twenties got off at Rowley Regis, glanced and gave me an inviting smile, though I am convinced she will give up on me soon. This is probably the lowest point of my life, maybe a change of job or a change of scenery was what I needed. I will probably have no choice at the end of the month.

When I finally found a seat, two middle aged men in suits were sitting opposite me, chatting about horse racing. They got off at the next station on route. I noticed a bulging manila envelope stuffed in the gap at the edge of the seat where the older men had been sitting. After looking around to check none of the commuter's eyes had strayed from their newspapers or books that served to help them to escape from their mundane daily journeys, I swapped seats and discreetly pulled out the envelope.

Slipping the packet into my pocket, I immediately made my way to the toilet. Squeezing through the small door and managing to turn around with my backpack on. Locking the door in such a cramped space was a miracle in itself. I dared not move left or right for fear of flushing the toilet or kick-starting the hand dryer. I sat on the toilet seat and pulled the package from my pocket. It was thick and heavy. I opened it neatly from the one edge and pulled out a polythene bag containing cash. The used notes were folded and inside it there was a key, with a similar fob to those used in hotels before plastic door cards became fashionable. I put the key back in the envelope and counted the cash quickly. A thousand pounds in £20 notes and £9,000 in £50s. My heart started racing, I could feel it pulsating all round my body. Within seconds I felt hot and started sweating and my hands had started to shake. I had never been lucky and finding a wad of cash made me both excited and dumbstruck. I was almost in a daze. But managed to hide my bounty carefully. Sweat started running into my eyes, though I knew it was not that hot. Someone banged the door and I told them the toilet was occupied. It took a further two minutes for me to return to a state calm enough to leave the security and stench of the cramped toilet. I nodded to a teenage lad standing directly outside the door who was hopping from one foot to another.

Chapter Three

The rain stopped as I walked the short distance to my flat from Kidderminster station. I crossed over Station Hill and resisted the call from the Railway Bell on the corner, an ideal pub to drown my sorrows when the funds were in place. Instead, I walked down the street adjacent to the Railway Bell, packed with terraced houses on either side. My place was the bottom half of a two up, two-down house halfway down the street. Not a great place to live. The plan was to move out at the end of my lease in five-months' time – if I was still in work. Sitting at a small table in the dimly lit kitchen I emptied the package. The pile of red and purple used notes brought a smile to my face, the metal fob and key created intrigue. I took a minute to stare, for no good reason, probably as it was the first time, I had handled that amount of money. Notes were counted into £500 stacks, taking one note from each stack and folding it the opposite way to keep them together.

Close inspection of ten of the notes did not give me reason to panic, but I wanted to know for sure if they were real. You often heard of counterfeit £50 notes. I opened my laptop and Google came up with a number of current fake note images – none of which applied to my newly found treasure. The haul less £500, went back in the original packaging, then in a resealable food bag that I placed in the back of the freezer. According to American TV movies, it is one of the first places a visiting burglar checks, but options were limited in my cramped little apartment. Hopefully burglars would not be visiting my grubby flat and if they did, they never had time to waste on American TV movies. I sat down and could feel my heart racing again, this time my hands decided to join the party and shook uncontrollably for a few minutes.

After some newly invented breathing exercises, normality returned. I picked up the key. Beaumont Hotel, Room 14 was printed in blue text on the chrome fob. I found the hotel online; it was around a mile from where I worked, near the city centre. The street view showed the hotel in a row of white painted four-story Edwardian dwellings, exclusive buildings in their day. So, what do I do now? There is no way I would surrender my haul to the police. My slice of luck was long overdue. The key is a different matter, do I throw it in the bin or find the lock that it fits. When I thought about it, I had to ask myself, had I become Peter Pan retrieving the key from Captain Hook to free Tinkerbell. I must be going mad - I could not think straight. I have just been gifted ten grand and should be happy - instead, my brain felt washed out and drained. I needed to erase the cash and key from my mind for a while before I went completely mad. I grabbed my coat and walked round the corner to Station Hill in search of a takeaway curry and a bottle of wine, courtesy of one of the newly found notes.

Chapter Four

Saturday morning arrived and before my caffeine fix, I knew I would be heading into the city again. I had decided to pander to my curiosity and see where the key would take me. In truth, it was always going to happen

Sitting back, I enjoyed the luxury of a half empty carriage. In the week, the journey was standing room only for at least the last 12 miles. It was my intention to relax without a care in the world, but my mind kept wandering to the key kept safely zipped in my jacket. After a few miles of farm fields and woods the landscape changed with dull, dirty factories and warehouses on either side of the rail lines, accompanied by the pungent and distinctive smell of the Accles and Pollock chemical plant. The train chugged on ploughing a trail between the ugly buildings of the West Midlands industrial heartlands until reaching the outskirts of Birmingham. The Victorian city had plenty of dull 60s and 70s low and high-rise buildings, but as I walked from Snow Hill station in Birmingham's financial quarter, huge gleaming office blocks breathed down on me. It took me less than ten minutes to walk to my destination.

Chapter Five

S tanding in front of the building I could see basement
properties below the cast iron railings. Four large steps led
up to a huge traditional black Georgian style door that was ajar.
I walked through the door carrying on a further three yards
further in, before finding myself in a hall with a tall ceiling and
simple décor. I presumed this place catered for permanent
guests rather than acting as a hotel these days. A faded sign at
the bottom of the stairs with carved wood bannisters said 7 –
20 and I followed the subsequent signs making my way to the
second floor. The landing had a damp pungent smell, like an
old flannel. It appeared that the days of this place being a hotel
were long over and it had now become budget rooms in a
building that lacked maintenance.

Room 14 was like any of the others in the corridor with a
buff door in need of repainting, a black doorknob, and a Yale
lock above it. I knocked the door, looking around for reactions
from the neighbours. The second knock was also fruitless and
failed to disturb anyone on the corridor. I turned the key slowly
and took three steps inside. The door slammed behind me. I
looked ahead. The wall in front was white without windows.
So were the walls to my right and left. The ceiling and floor
were the same colour. I turned around looking where I had
entered and walked back to the door. The old handle did not

move. The door was firmly locked. I shook it and shook it for around a minute before it came off in my hand.

Banging hard on all the walls screaming "help, get me out", achieved nothing. Sweat started to pour from my forehead and within three minutes my hoodie was soaking wet. I thought someone was playing a joke on me or were there ten thousand reasons to lock me in this room? Music played loudly from an adjacent room. It was strange. I had heard it before but could not recognise it. I then realised it was The Zorba, Greek music I had seen men and women dance to at a wedding of one of Angie's friends about a year ago. Another round of screams with bangs on the door and walls brought no success. I sat on the floor. Though I really did want to act like a blubbering schoolboy, I told myself I should be strong. The message failed to reach my body. My hands, and legs shook vigorously. Someone inside my head decided to play the bass drum. Twelve of his friends joined in within a minute.

After about an hour, the door flung open. It was a stocky Latin looking middle aged man. "Stay on the floor," he said pointing a revolver at me. A revolver – this is Birmingham not Miami – what have I got myself into?

"You have two choices. Do a job, keep the money and get more money, or die. Make your choice?"

"What job?"

"That doesn't matter – live or die?"

I did not hesitate. I had decided there was no way I could buy time with this guy. He was not a great conversationalist, and his proposal was not supported with a sales pitch – it was live or die. Take it or leave it.

"Live."

He nodded his head.

"Are you Greek I asked?"

"Yes – but this has nothing to do with Greeks. These people are fierce – they will kill you without a thought. If it goes wrong, they will kill me. They are not Greek."

The door slammed shut.

About two hours later a small portable toilet, a bowl of water, soap and a microwave meal were delivered by Zorba the Brummie. The curry and rice smelt good even though it was a supermarket meal for one. I gobbled it down at a rapid pace – I had not eaten for a while. Before the last morsel of food went in, I felt extremely tired, dropped the plastic fork and my eyes refused to open. I was squatting on the floor eating but fell to one side with the side of my face pressed against the cold floor.

When I woke up, I had no idea how long I had been asleep. My clothes had disappeared, I was naked apart from my boxer shorts. Fresh underwear, socks, shoes, a white shirt, and a grey suit were folded in a corner of the room. Sometime later my Greek mate pushed the door open pointing his gun at me. He placed a laptop bag on the ground.

"You've got an easy job my friend," he said in a quiet tone. "Deliver that bag to an address in London – to a man by the name of John Manchester. To him and him alone."

He took out a white envelope from his trouser pocket and threw it on the floor.

"There is a £1,000 in cash, a credit card, remember code 9264 and the address for the delivery is on the envelope. Do not open the bag."

He walked out and left the door open this time, but I could not work out where he went to. I washed in the same water again and put on the clothes. Shirt, suit, shoes all fitted perfectly. That was worrying. Do they know everything about me, where I live, what I do, or when I passed out due to the dodgy curry did Zorba measure me up and pop to Marks and Spencer's? I wasn't sweating, nor was my heart racing, but I was scared. This was all new to me and I had never been scared like this before. What are they doing to me? The only answer I had was that they had gone to all this trouble to deliver a package that was highly illegal putting my life in danger or offering the prospect of being apprehended and jailed.

I crossed the road and walked down a Victorian upmarket shopping arcade where middle-aged women were mesmerised by the window displays before entering shops and spending more on ornaments than I earned in a month. In less than ten minutes, I was in Birmingham's main railway station, New Street. I tried the credit card out, as I did not know its limit or even if it would be declined. A first-class ticket to London Euston was booked and the credit card was debited immediately. I had 20 minutes before the train left and quickly demolished a burger washing it down with a diet drink before heading to the platform and my first-class carriage. I wanted the luxury of the best seats if someone else was paying, but primarily I thought the privacy might be useful.

A brunette hostess dressed in a red blouse and black skirt with tied up shiny dark hair welcomed me and showed me to my seat. She could easily have been strutting the catwalk instead of walking up and down the first-class aisles.

"Would you like anything to eat or drink?" the woman asked with a well-practiced smile. "I could do with a coffee and a snack."

The offer of Danish pastries brought a smile to my face.

"Anything else you might be needing?"

"There is one thing. I have lost my phone and I need to find the place I'm staying. Do you have such a relic as a London map?"

"No, I don't, but I can bring you an iPad out."

I knew there was a reason for travelling first class. The hostess also bought The Daily Telegraph and The Mirror out with the pastries and a cafetière of coffee, but my priority was to find out where I was going.

Chapter Six

Hotel Earle, Sussex Place, Paddington, London, W2 2TP was typed on the envelope. It was easily found on Google Maps, five-minutes' walk from Paddington Station. Another old white hotel in the middle of a row of hotels. This one looked and sounded from recent online comments I had read on TripAdvisor that it was open for business. I picked up The Mirror and realised it was Monday, which means I had arrived in Birmingham Saturday morning and left on Monday morning – the drugs in that dodgy curry must have been good. As usual I looked at the sports first. The back page lead had United linked with another £300,000 a week footballer – the other big story implied Spurs will be looking for a new manager. Those headlines could have been written any week of the season and I soon turned inside to learn my team had won on Saturday, though the Albion had built me up and let me down so many times I was getting immune to talk of success or failure.

The front pages were full of politics, plus there was another drone causing havoc at an airport – this time Cardiff. I got to page 11, and I gulped leaving my mouth open and my chin near the table. 'Suspicious Deaths Linked' was the headline on the edge of the page. A man in his 30s had been found dead in a hotel in West London. Police refused to rule out links to two other suspicious deaths at hotels in different parts of

London. They were all well dressed in suits and similar ages. All three photos of the men had been published in a bid for them to be identified. They looked my age and none of them were carrying ID. There were too many coincidences with my plight and guess what I'm heading to a London hotel. I ripped through the Daily Telegraph and found 'West London Death Suspicious' with a less dramatic more matter of fact report printed with the same images.

I could feel my pulse racing through my neck, a sick feeling in my stomach accompanied another breakout of sweat. I could not be sure that these three died at the hands of the same people who had drugged me and sent me to London, but there were too many coincidences. My mind firmly believed the same killers were on my case and I was frightened. I got up and walked to the back of the carriage and found the hostess taking a break.

"Thanks for the use of the iPad, I desperately need to make a call – do you have a phone I could use?"

"We don't. I probably shouldn't tell you this, but the iPads have SIM cards fitted, and you can make a call with them. You are just going to dial a UK mobile or landline I presume?"

"Well, I thought about calling my cousin in Belize, "I said with a smirk. Trying to be clever without succeeding. "No, you're right I'm only calling a UK mobile. You are terrific. Thanks"

"They all say that, but never offer to take me out."

My heart was still beating rapidly, but now my face was hot and probably red in embarrassment to accompany the sweats. I recovered with a quick question, though still stunned that she was asking for a date. Straight out, there and then.

"So, if I asked you out, would you say yes?"

"I'll give you my number."

"I'm really flattered. My name's Paul. I should be back in about a week. Are you based in Birmingham or London?" I replied as my confidence grew and my face cooled.

"Either. Let's meet up."

Chapter Seven

The news of the three deaths had been tempered by the interest of a woman who was not just out of my league, in football terms she was an international willing to mix with a part time player. On other occasions interest from Michelle, well that was the name she had written down, would have made me feel like I was walking on the moon, but today I was more worried about staying alive here on earth and living until the end of the day.

Taking out Michelle was a thought that stayed with me, though my mind was running overtime. What's going on? Why would she want to be seen with me? Is there something more sinister going on? I convinced myself I was being stupid. Not so much because I could use clear logic to dismiss my fears more the fact that I desperately wanted to see this woman again and I was prepared to take a risk.

I had grown up with Gary Parsons. We had remained mates through thick and thin. His number was one of the few I could remember, and I called him on the iPad.

"Gazzer. Alright mate."

"Yea – where have you been Paul?"

"It's really complicated mate. Are you working round Kiddy again and still got me key?" "Yea."

I looked around the carriage to check there was still no one in earshot.

"OK. I want you to go around the flat now. There is a plastic bag with cash in it at the back of the freezer – I want you to get that bag, my passport and cheque book from my bedside table and take them to your house. Can you do that now Gazzer?"

"Course mate. Yea. But you don't sound right. This is really weird."

"Trust me Gaz – I need your help."

"It's done mate."

"I can't ring you until I get a phone – just borrowed this."

"Good luck mate."

After ending the call, I just stared at the iPad for no reason. After ten minutes I got it together again. These guys were murdered because they did not do what they were told or whoever is behind this operation murders the couriers at the first opportunity because they want no loose ends. Do I make a run for it now or do I deliver and split? The one hour, 26-minute journey was already an hour underway, so I had to make my mind up quickly.

Deliver and split was the decision.

The split was the hard decision. No ID, no passport. I thought I had to stay in Britain or risk the ferry to Ireland. No way could I fly to Spain or anywhere. I had travelled on the ferry a couple of times on lads' weekends away without being asked for identification – it seemed a good bet as did the Welsh coast where I would fit in with the thousands of folks from the West Midlands on holiday, living or working the summer. I opened the iPad again and discovered I could head to the Dublin ferry from Holyhead port in Anglesey with a direct train from Euston. I had yet to decide whether Ireland was my destination. Should I decide against it, I would head for the Welsh coast and the mid-Wales stretch was not too far off route.

Chapter Eight

The train rolled into Euston. I folded the iPad cover up and headed to the rear of the carriage. I felt uncomfortable speaking to Michelle again. I had never dated a woman as beautiful as her. Her smile negated all the shy and inferior feelings I felt, and I responded with puppy dog eyes and a look that could only say 'please let me be lucky enough to meet up with you again one day'.

"I don't ask guys out usually – please don't let me down," she pleaded and handed me a note.

I nodded and walked off the train onto the platform thinking 'why is she even looking at me?' I hoped that one day we would meet again – but I knew dreams rarely came true. Never had a woman made an instant impression on me and why, oh why, had it not happened on any other day in my pathetic life?

Chapter Nine

The credit card I was given was probably being monitored. I reckon that any transactions would be available to them within a couple of hours, possibly a few minutes. Guessing the maximum cash withdrawal was £300, I joined a small queue at the first group of ATMs I spotted and was successful in increasing my traveling fund. I walked out of the station and spotted another Big Issue salesman. There were three rough sleepers close by – all of them had glazed eyes and ready to sleep. Another homeless guy 20-yards further down was younger than me and appeared bright wearing a recent change of clothes. Just the man I was looking for.

"It's your lucky day mate."

"Eh."

"Put this in your pocket and remember the PIN 9264. You can spend on it today without any problems and draw £300 a day from tomorrow onwards. 9264 – got it?"

"Ah, good man – bless yer."

If it goes to plan that card would be leading my mysterious gang of crooks a dance. They will think I am still in London when I am miles away.

Chapter Ten

I walked back into the station and down the ramp to the line of taxis and asked the first driver on the rank to take me straight to the hotel. I got out with the bag, asked the driver to wait for me and then walked straight to reception.

A dark-haired middle-aged woman in uniform looked down at a computer screen without acknowledging I was there. Eventually she raised her head.

"I am here to see a man by the name of John Manchester."

"No meeting requests for anyone of that name," she said in an East European accent. "Let me check hotel guest list."

"No. No one by that name."

"Could one of your colleagues have taken a message? How long have you been here?" "I've been here since six – I'll call the only other person who might know."

She picked up the phone and said: "Ludvik, man here to meet a Mr. Manchester. Know anything?"

She put the phone down and said: "No one here and no messages from man." "Thank you – I'll pop back later."

"Whatever."

Chapter Eleven

There was no way I would return to the budget hotel in Paddington, I needed to keep one step ahead of those murdering bastards and instructed the driver to go to Euston, explaining we needed to stop at a mobile phone on the way. I opened the laptop bag against Zorba's orders. There seemed to be just packaging at the top, nothing I could make out without emptying the bag. It could be bugged; Zorba could have put a tracker in the lining. I thought about leaving it in the taxi, but if it were bugged, they would know the first stop was Euston. I must leave it at, or near the phone shop.

The geeky kid behind the counter said the best deal would be a Samsung phone that looked easy enough to operate and I put £50 credit on it, though I planned not to use it much. Just to check out train times, ferries and make a few calls.

"I can't remember the last time someone came in here and wanted to pay cash," said the assistant looking over his rounded spectacles. "You robbed a bank, or won't anyone give you a credit card?"

"No, you cheeky snot gobbler – the last shop I didn't like the bloke's attitude, so I knocked him out and nicked his cash."

So much for me being discreet and not leaving a footprint. After a short nervous laugh, the geek shut up. The bag was at my feet whilst I stood at the counter, that is where it stayed. I jumped back in the black cab and headed for Euston.

Chapter Twelve

The single to Holyhead was paid for in cash and there was a direct train every hour, the next one would probably be busy. During the next couple of hours, I would decide whether to go to Ireland or get off before the train reaches Anglesey. It would be leaving in around 15 minutes, so I made my way towards platform 18 and the peasant class seat was a luxury opposed to staying at manic Euston for one more minute than I needed. I added a can of coke, a two-litre bottle of water and a large bar of Cadbury's Whole Nut to my limited travelling kit and waited patiently at the platform. Some new clothes were needed, but the most important action was my need to get out of London. There was only a few more minutes left to wait, yet I was getting more and more anxious. I kept looking up and down the platform in search of anyone that looked slightly suspicious. My heart was racing again. I was on edge and felt uncomfortable. No one knew I was here, so why was I worrying. I needed the train to arrive so I could get onboard and relax.

The train pulled in and people got off whilst all those people relaxing on benches, standing and reading newspapers or drinking coffee suddenly sprang into action. They hustled and pushed to be one of the first to enter their chosen carriage. I got on near the rear of the train and sat in a window seat in what I hoped to be a forward-facing seat. When I had placed my small amount of traveling goods exactly where I wanted them, I scanned the other seats to see if I had anyone tailing me. Not that I could spot a villain who specialized in killing young men in down market hotels or how a sinister criminal might dress.

There was a group of seven females at the far end of my carriage. I soon discovered they were Travellers, probably on their way to Ireland. They were loud at times and under the influence of the bottles each of them appeared to stow in their handbags, but they caused no harm. No worse than any group of women on their travels and mild in comparison to a bunch of peroxide blondes with £25 nails, wild and fearless on hen trips, where it just so happened one of them looked even sillier with a sash and a homemade hat. A man in his 60s sat quietly halfway down the carriage dressed in white shirt and black tie, probably returning from laying a friend to rest. He stared at the floor with empty eyes.

Though I felt more relaxed than when I was tearing around London, it was not long before I was thinking about the bad guys. If all three were males and my age, what happened to the women or older men who had picked up a package. Were they not allowed to get near the hotel in Birmingham or were they murdered? Thinking about it. Could the two men who left the train before me on my way home from work have planted the package when they saw a suitable target? The phone was in my trouser pocket, digging into my thigh. Being on the run was affecting me, I did not know how long I could do this. The thought of people being murdered and my life under threat was worsened by the fact I did not know who was after me and what I had done to get involved in this mess. I wanted to phone

Michelle, Dad, and my best friend, but I knew now was not the time.

My heart missed a beat as a tall stocky man entered the carriage. I was frightened for my life because at first glance I thought it was Zorba. The man mountain made another couple of steps, and I realised he looked nothing like the Greek. I was living on my nerves, and it took very little to put me on edge.

First stop would be Milton Keynes and I had given myself a deadline. Decide where I am going before Crewe. I guessed that security would have tightened at the ports the last couple of years, but I would not get arrested for traveling without a passport – I could always jump back on a train. It was gamble. I had no contacts in Ireland and I knew the Welsh coast better than the Emerald Isle. I had been to Dublin twice, smashed when I got there, hungover when I departed. Plan B was to alight at ether Prestatyn, Rhyl, Colwyn Bay, Llandudno Junction or Bangor.

The guard came along and checked my ticket. Half an hour later I had a coffee. The old man in the black tie lined up a couple of drinks, that appeared to be whiskey – he kept his head bowed. The group of ladies ordered cokes, to compliment the spirits in their bags which would be making an appearance as soon as the drink and beverage trolley was in the next carriage.

I had decided. Well, I had come up with a plan that had two or three scenarios. I would get off at Prestatyn, though my destination was Barmouth or somewhere not too far away on the coast. I could carry on in the direction of the mid-Wales coast or stay in Prestatyn for a night or two or jump back on the train later and head for Llandudno, where I had previously spent three short breaks. It was a pity my plan had so many ifs, buts and maybes.

I got up to get off the train at Prestatyn and walked past the travellers.

"You can't go – you haven't said hello to us. Come and have a drink, you can sit on my lap," said a slim girl in her mid-20s.

"He's alright him. I could take him home," an older hard-faced woman in the group said to the accompaniment of laughter from each and every one of them.

"Sorry ladies, I can't stop – maybe another day."

"We didn't intend to be ladies if you joined us."

"Ha – Mary would ride him on the train."

"You young 'uns didn't invent it."

I forced a grin, jumped off onto the platform and decided I had just experienced a lucky escape from the man-eaters.

Chapter Thirteen

Food was top of the agenda again and I planned to eat at a well-mannered pace this time. I decided not to head for food immediately. For around ten-minutes, I sat on a bench just in case someone was tailing me. Not many people were around, and it seemed no one was interested in me, so I walked in a straight line from the station towards the beach which was half a mile away. Past the inevitable caravan site on the left and a quaint looking park on the right. There was a café just past the park on a road on the right before I got to the beach. I walked through the door, that appeared permanently ajar and could not avoid the noise coming from a pair of spoilt kids at a table near the door, whose parents were zoned out and totally oblivious to their youngsters. The adults were eating breakfast. That would do for me.

"What can I get yer luv?" said the young girl with a strong Liverpool accent.

"I'll take a full breakfast with toast and a tea, nice and strong, splash of milk. Can you do us a favour? Can I have runny eggs and burnt sausage, no tomatoes please?"

"Not that you are fussy," she said with a grin.

Ten minutes later she called out: "Breakfast and tea for fussy man."

I smiled walked to the counter and picked the tea up with my left hand and the plate with my other and turned. As I turned, I walked straight into a woman, pouring boiling tea all down her sweater. I could not avoid the piercing look of a warrior who gave me the impression she would always choose to fight before considering any other options.

"You fecking eejit. Yer gobshite," the redhead shouted.

If I was a foot closer, I am sure she would have knocked me out. She had the look in her eyes. I had picked the wrong woman to spill my tea down.

"I'm really sorry – I am so stupid."

"You're not wrong there."

"Come out the back love – we'll sort you out," said the girl at the counter who handed her over to another woman who must have been the cook.

I put my breakfast down and returned to the counter with my empty mug. "Can I get you something to eat or drink?" I shouted out.

"I'll have a breakfast and a tea, eejit," the redhead replied.

I got myself another tea and paid for the wild woman's breakfast.

"Not too fussy who you who you throw your tea over, are yer?"

"Why is it that every Scouser I have ever met thinks they are a comedian?"

"Yea and I suppose not all Brummies' are thick, are they?"

"I'm not a Brummie."

"Could have fooled me – you are not too bright, are you?"

At that, I gave in, conceding defeat.

Returning to my table I got stuck into my breakfast, as if I had not eaten for a week. Plans to eat a well-mannered pace were soon forgotten and the redhead returned in dry sweatshirt five minutes later when I had almost demolished my breakfast. She was wearing a pair of shorts and a sweatshirt, carrying her wet clothes in a supermarket carrier bag. Her milky white legs and freckles did not detract from her natural beauty – in fact the freckles were a bonus in my eyes.

"Can we start again?"

"That will be grand, but anything like that happens you will need to be able to run very, very quickly," she replied with a wry smile.

"I'm Paul."

"Aislinn."

The redhead mimicked my accent and made me feel like an idiot.

"Hi... Hi Paul."

She shook her head, I didn't respond.

Chapter Fourteen

In between the remaining mouthfuls that I chewed slowly in Aislinn's presence, I learned that she was living in a caravan north of Barmouth and had two jobs. She had come over from Ireland the previous summer as well.

"So, you know all about me, what are you doing here – or do you travel Britain throwing tea all over folk?"

"I'm looking to get away and work on the coast for the summer – I lost my job in Birmingham. Life was going from bad to worse back home, so I thought I'd give it a go round here. We had loads of holidays out here when I was a kid and I loved it.

"Come with me, I'll find you a job."

"Serious?"

"Yea – stop at my place until you're on yer feet – I'll get you work in three days."

I could not believe my luck. Scold a pretty woman who nearly knocks me out before taking pity on me, promises to get me a job and puts me up at her place. I was tempted to pinch myself but decided my body had put up with enough pain and abuse the last few days. I said goodbye to the Scouser who appeared amazed to see me leaving with Aislinn.

"Careful how you go," she said. "Your luck has to run out sooner or later." If only she knew the truth.

Chapter Fifteen

We jumped into an old red Ford Fiesta with Galway license plates. It struggled to start.

"Come on ye auld scut," she shouted. The Fiesta heard her and fired into life before cruising along without a care in the world.

"Is there somewhere I could stop to get some clothes – don't feel good in a suit?"

"No. Let's stop at another café and I'll throw a cup of tea over your suit – you might feel more comfortable then," she said with a smile. "Don't worry I've got some clothes she can have, though I must agree, you don't look good in a suit."

I was grateful but couldn't resist questioning the redhead: "Thanks. Am I the same size as an old boyfriend?"

"He wasn't that old – same age as me. You want to know it all don't yer? You will be asking about my distant relatives, my first pet and the family name of my priest next."

"Why not?"

"Well not everyone wants to spew out all their personal information and past to someone they just met, but I will tell you before you get too upset. Last spring, I came over here with a guy I was at uni with. He didn't last the summer, but some of his clothes did. I've got the same caravan this summer and the same stupid sweatshirts, tracky bottoms and polo shirts are still in the cupboard. No footwear I'm afraid. You will have to make do with those executive loafers. Anyway, we know how nimble on your toes you are when you wear them."

She was not going to let it go. I expected to be reminded of my carelessness with a cuppa forever afterwards. I was expecting it. In fact, I was looking forward to more banter. She was a good person to be around with her cute freckles and sardonic humour, but I best not cross her as she looked capable of changing from Snow White to Godzilla in seconds.

We did not drive through Barmouth, but were not too far away. She pulled off the main road and crossed over a railway track. I could see the sea in the distance and as always, I lost over 20-years for a moment or two and became a little boy amazed at the sight of the blue expanse in front of me. I used to tell myself that one day I would live by the sea – maybe this was the opportunity to move on and start a new life somewhere.

There was a pub on the right of the narrow lane before we came to a large caravan site on the left. It appeared to be a private site with just electricity feeds, no shop and thankfully no amusement arcade. I helped Aislinn in with a couple of bags of shopping she had picked up earlier in the day.

Chapter Sixteen

"We've got some fish in the freezer and I'll do some mashed potato," she said. "That would be great," I replied not telling her I was not too keen on mash. "Could really do with getting cleaned up – been in this gear since Saturday morning."

"There is a shower on the right there, knock yourself out. Here's a towel – I'll sort something out for you to wear whilst you shower."

Knocking myself out in this old caravan was a distinct possibility in the shower room. There was no more room than a train toilet. I could just turn around and I am not packing any extra pounds. At least the water was warm, and I would soon smell human again. There was three days beard growth, that would have to go into four days and possibly more, but I could put up with that after the challenges of the last few days.

"There's some clothes on the bed in my room."

"You're a darling Aislinn. Do you fancy a drink at the pub after tea?

She smiled when I used the word tea and nodded her head.

"I will go out and be seen with yer – as long as you don't start throwing yer beer about eejit."

I chose jeans over tracksuit bottoms. Could be my age or that I am a bit of a snob, but I would never wear 'trackies' if I went out of the house. Lots of people do these days. It just reminds me of guys striding around with their big heavy necklaces that must leave them with a permanent stoop. The jeans were a bit long, but fitted round my waist. There were T-shirts, socks and boxers – I chose a black University College Dublin sweatshirt. It did not feel right wearing another man's boxers, but I had little choice.

After we had eaten, I washed up whilst Aislinn made up a bed at the end of the caravan in front of a large window.

"Right, that's you then. Give me half hour and I'll be ready"

"OK. I'm going to walk down to the sea."

"Have you got your water wings Paul. Bet yer mammy wouldn't let you go on yer own."

The wind howled across the beach. It was cool, but exhilarating. There is something magical about walking on the beach and watching the waves crashing in. As a youngster I would head off for hours climbing, exploring rock pools, and running through the waves. We had our share of rain on Welsh caravan holidays, but it was a world apart from the Black Country until you bumped into some of the miserable old couples who travel down regularly moaning the Welsh are ripping them off and keep telling everyone how good it is back home. I could have stayed on the beach longer, but the lady from across the sea is waiting. I cannot believe she has been so good to me and find it hard to understand she is not involved with a man. I kept telling myself that I must not make any advances – that might ruin everything.

Chapter Seventeen

We waked through the pub entrance and into and made our way towards a large bar on the right. A young barman smiled at Aislinn.

"Brought another Paddy in to tell us how good you lot are at rugby?"

"No. He's a Brummie."

"I'm not a Brummie."

"No Ash. He's a Yam, Yam. I can tell."

"I can't tell the difference. They're all as thick as shite," she said with a grin.

I have travelled the country and put up with thick Brummie jibes. More abuse from these pair would not have the slightest effect.

"When you opened your mouth I could tell instantly you were a Yam Yam, it was the sweatshirt that made me think you were a Paddy."

"He's wearing some of Liam's old clothes. Well, everything he is wearing is Liam's including his kecks."

The barman shook his head. My face turned red with embarrassment. "You must be very poor, desperate or have some sort of twisted sexual perversions.

"No mate, just got out of the shower and had no clean clothes of my own. The barman grimaced and held his hands out in front of him."

"What are you drinking then?"

"I'll take a bottle of Magners."

"How about our latest visitor?"

Welsh beer had not always been kind, so I was glad to see a Marston's Pedigree pull. I pointed at the pump.

"Pint of Pedigree please."

Aislinn took a long swig from the bottle and said: "Gareth, Paul. Paul, Gareth." We shook hands. Gareth seemed friendly enough.

"So, what's the connection between you two then?"

"The Brummie threw a cup of tea over me in Prestatyn – we've been best friends ever since. I said I would find him some work."

"There's a couple of shifts coming up here and lots of work in Barmouth now it's getting busier. Mind you, I don't know if a good pub like this that the locals drink in, could cope with a Paddy and a Yam, Yam on the same shift, though I'd be more worried about you pair wearing clean kecks."

"This is one of my three jobs," explained Aislinn. "I sort the caravans out and also help an old lady about half a mile up the road."

"A right Florence Nightingale," I said, grasping one of few opportunities to poke fun at the Irish woman.

"It's Doctor Kathleen Lynn, if you're having the craic. She wouldn't put up with any shite from you English either."

What the hell she was rambling on about went straight over my head, but the way she responded with her easy anti-English put down brought a smile to my face.

An old man said hello to Aislinn and Gareth before making his way to the bottom of the room where he joined a group speaking Gaelic. In this area they were proud Welsh men and women but realised the English mainly from the West Midlands and North West were no longer their enemies and the few occasions I had joined a Welsh speaking group they always reverted to English. It was an accepted fact that thousands of caravaners and renters of cottages and flats would descend each year and any hostilities had long gone. In fact, it has been a while since the Sons of Glydwr were setting fire to English owned homes in this part of the world and they were never interested in caravans anyway.

I bought another round of drinks and thought to myself, I am relaxed, and it is a long time since I have been so happy. Why? Like the three males who died, I had no identification, sent to London, similar age – someone wants me dead. And I am relaxed and happy. You're a sick man Ellis. It could be because I am by the sea and with a woman who I seem to have some chemistry. Or maybe I am mad, and I like running around the place avoiding someone I have never met who wants to kill me.

Four pints later, I still have a way to go before the drink would knock me over, but the strain of the last few days is getting to me, and I am exhausted.

"Shall we get you to bed Brummie?"

"That's an offer you can't refuse," chirped Gareth.

"It's not like that," I protested. "She's my saviour in shining armour – rescued me like a female Liam Neeson."

"Get to bed yer drunken Bollocks – he's an auld granda' anyway."

When she turned and headed for the door, I looked at Gareth who had a huge grin on his face. He held his two hands above his head and created the heart sign Taylor Swift made famous, before winking at me. I was not convinced that love had made it as far as this part of Wales let alone big bruising Welsh guys becoming familiar with Taylor Swift.

Chapter Eighteen

I caught up with Aislinn as she exited the pub and managed to walk in a straight line down the dark lane to the site. I had enjoyed a few beers and would be asleep as soon as my head hit the pillow of my sofa converted to a bed.

Aislinn turned left when she entered the caravan, and I went right as though she was at the top of the steps boarding a transatlantic flight heading for business class whilst I headed for coach.

"Goodnight Brummie."

"Night Doc."

Five minutes later Aislinn had taken her clothes off, walked from her room and joined me in bed. I might be in a battered old caravan, but there was nowhere in the world I would rather be at this moment. I could just catch her smirk in the dark as her freckles glowed against her curly red hair. It was a waste of time trying to be cool – I starred at Aislinn with the grin of a lottery winner.

"So, you're the doctor and I'm the patient - yea."

"Shut the fuck up."

Chapter Nineteen

I woke up to the smell of bacon frying. The grin that had invaded and conquered my face when Aislinn jumped into my bed was still there, but my body was now so relaxed, getting out of bed was going to be a major effort. Lying close to Aislinn and giving each other exactly what we wanted and needed was without doubt the best night I had ever had. The aches and pains from my back and shoulders due to the hard surface would not deter from that 'good to be alive' feeling.

"Coffee Brummie?"

"Please. Pretty good service here. Fresh clothes, night on the beer and breakfast with a smile.

"Plus, the best time I've ever had overnight," I added sheepishly.

"Who said you are getting breakfast? Yea, last night had its moments, but if you are expecting me to tell you how good you were, you've come to the wrong girl. And you should have guessed by now, I don't like any of that mushy shite."

I replied attempting to mimic a posh public schoolboy.

"Never mind. If I could just place on record that I had a wonderful evening."

I thought she was going to smile. Her face betrayed her for a few milliseconds and then she barked at me.

"Just get some clothes on, I'm dishing the bacon up. The last thing I want to see is your micky over the table when I'm eating breakfast."

We ate in silence and the coffee brought me out of my daze. Aislinn told me she had to look after the old lady this morning and would be back around two. Dressed down in jeans and another university sweatshirt, she bid goodbye and drove off in the Fiesta after three attempts to get it started. No kiss on the cheek, affectionate embrace or even an arm across my shoulder. It was though last night never happened. To me it was a dream – to her it might have been a nightmare. I could not tell from her actions. In the short time I had known her, Aislinn had not been one for cosying up and was more at home with sniping put down remarks and sarcasm. I hoped it was a case that she was impressed with me but felt embarrassed to show it. Only time will tell, and she was worth persevering with.

Chapter Twenty

Not too much for me to do in the caravan, but the sea was close enough. What more does anyone want in life? I headed for the sea and within 100 yards I was stopped by a lonely old man with a springer spaniel who wanted a chat. I soon discovered he lived within five miles of where I was brought up and claimed to have worked with my uncle at a foundry. Like most of the old guys he reckoned he had one of the best 'vans' on the plot and wanted me to see it. I made my excuses, but he insisted I call in for a cup of tea on my way back. Old Joe had lost his wife a couple of years ago, he kept busy, but it was sad to see him going through the motions without his lifelong partner. I offered to take his dog Libby down to the sea, but Joe said the old dog had done enough for today. It was nice to chat, but I really liked walking solo with the wind blowing through my ears and the taste of salt at the back of my mouth. It had started to rain, but I didn't care. I walked for a further hour, as an adult I was still amazed how the waves came crashing in. If I could do this every day, I would not want for much more. Maybe some red-haired beauty with an attitude to go home to would complete the dream.

On the way back I called into Joe's place. He brought out tea and biscuits and I knew I would not get out of his caravan anytime soon. We did a tour of the Black Country and found another of my relatives he knew. I avoided telling him too many details from my recent escapades, but explained I moved in with Ash yesterday and she was finding me some work.

Joe had seen her behind the bar.

"Nice girl – looks alright as well," he said. "I saw her with a Cockney, who was the other side of the bar about a month ago, though I haven't seen him again. Big bloke – a bit flash. Bit old for her I thought.

"Not her boyfriend?"

"No. Last year she was over with a lad. Nice kid. Liam, I think. He had top grades in pharmacology I thought he said. Mind you, means nothing to me, I worked in a foundry all my life. He went home a good month before her last summer. I asked her where he was, you would have thought I wanted her mums phone number. No way she would talk about it to me."

"She helps some old lady out too?"

"Not sure if she does now – I know she was working in a coffee shop in Barmouth."

Following a full review of Joe's married life and how long he had been holidaying in Wales, I made my excuses and headed for home. As promised Aislinn returned around two and had finished work for the day. She said she hoped to speak to the landlord at the pub in the morning to secure some work for me. I suggested we drive into Barmouth, and this evening's food would be my treat. I did not have enough money to sustain a life on the run, but it looks like I could live a low-cost life on the mid-Wales coast if Ash would put up with me.

We spent the afternoon drinking tea and chatting before showering. Again, no signs of affection from Aislinn and I thought I best bottle my emotions as they would not be welcome. They say men think with their genitals – not me. I fall in love instantly. I am surprised I have never proposed on the first date or discussed the ideal honeymoon on the second. Aislinn was a different character altogether. Hard and unemotional. I wondered whether she had always been like this or one of her ex's, possibly Liam, had hurt her. She did not appear to look as if she would recover any time soon. I got the feeling that I would not change her, we were opposites. Now is the time to man up. It would be no hardship to carry on like this. Intimate nights and days where we were just mates, her target for humour. I could think of worse scenarios and there was no one I would rather snuggle up to in a makeshift caravan bed.

Chapter Twenty-One

Aislinn walked out of her bedroom in another set of clothes. She was still dressed casually in jeans and a sweatshirt, though she had made the effort to add lipstick and curl her hair. She looked good, but I dare not tell her.

"You ready Brummie?"

"Yea."

"Okay – let's head for the Welsh riviera."

We jumped into the battered Fiesta. The car struggled into life eventually and we headed to Barmouth.

"I haven't put my evening dress on, and you've forgotten your tuxedo, so our choice of restaurants will be limited," she said.

"Where do you want to eat?"

"Not fussed. Just some café or pub will do me – don't you fancy anything?" "I love fish and chips by the sea, but we had fish last night."

"That's okay."

"There's a good chippy here. Eat in or shall we walk by the sea with chips?

"Yea - I could do with the walk"

"And we can walk back hand in hand with the waves crashing around us."

Aislinn laughed and said: "There's no way I will be seen holding your battered fish hand in public, yer gobshite."

I let my tongue loose but looks like I got away with it. Remember Paul, affection is a non-starter. There is nothing quite like fish beside the seaside, even though we had to make our way past the arcades, candy floss sellers and other tacky stores to get near the waves. We were silent as we walked to the sea. My loafers were looking worse for wear thanks to the salt water, but I would be ditching them at the first opportunity for something more comfortable. Nightfall was still a couple of hours away and we walked across the beach past the yacht club to the small harbour. I asked Aislinn if she was staying until September, but she was non-committal and avoided looking me in the eyes. I put my arm around her and was soon rebuffed.

"Look Paul, I'm not into that lovey sugary stuff at the best of times. We have only just met; I'm not going to start choosing my bridesmaids. Let's just see how it goes. We've had a laugh so far – don't spoil it."

Once more I'd got it wrong. I just cannot help myself. An hour ago, my brain was telling the rest of my sorry soul that I had to man up and what happens? I act like some pre-programmed lustful robot. No further words were said as we walked towards the beach. I was disappointed and wanted more than a causal relationship with Ash. Though there was still hope - she had not ruled it out. I am not sure if it was because of the trauma in Birmingham and London, the shock of finding someone willing to help me or simply the fact I had met a beautiful somewhat mysterious woman. It was clear I had fallen for her, but I needed to keep that to myself for a little while longer.

I broke the silence: "Fancy a drink?"

"Don't mind if I do Brummie boy. Shall we mix with the holidaymakers or get one nearer to home?"

"Whatever – you're the boss."

"We both know that you're wasting your words," she said with a smile.

Chapter Twenty-Two

Gareth was standing at the bar, without too much to do in the almost empty pub. "Got any work Yam Yam?" he asked.

"Ash is having a word with your boss in the morning."

"Didn't know David was working Wednesday – oh well, good luck."

"So that will be a pint of Pedigree and a bottle of mouldy Irish apple juice for the lady, sorry for Aislinn."

"Watch yer mouth gobshite. I am a lady who just has to sink down to your level, or shall I say the trough when I'm out with eejits like you pair."

We had a couple of drinks and I learned that Ash had a good knowledge of rugby, though her and Gareth failed to agree on a number of occasions. A local with a body like a weightlifter was soon sent packing when he dared to talk about how tough the Welsh are. She insisted that Welsh rugby players were like old women compared to the amateur Irish hurling and football players back home. The muscleman could not get a word in as Ash tore into him. After an hour we headed for the caravan. She did not bid me goodnight this evening just ditched her clothes and jumped into my bed with me.

Chapter Twenty-Three

The next morning Aislinn was up first again. I got a mumbled "morning" as I headed for the shower. I put some fresh boxers on along with a T shirt plus the jeans and hoodie I had worn yesterday. I squeezed into the only footwear I had as I planned another walk.

Walking into the kitchen she greeted me with: "I'm going to the pub, I'll get some bacon and will be back in the next hour or so. I have not made you a coffee, but here's a juice Brummie. I sat on the bed and drank the orange. She said goodbye as I put the glass on the table and within 20 seconds my head was spinning. I had been drugged. I was positive about it. It was less than three yards to the kitchen sink, it felt like 100 yards. My head fell into the sink, my forehead bouncing off the aluminum - It was a major effort to lift my head, but I did and shoved my fingers down my throat. I was sick, but still felt dizzy and very weak. I took a mug half filled it with water from the kettle and another inch of cold water. I must have put five or six tablespoons of salt in the mug before stirring it. I knew I had to something to stay alive – I downed it one. It did the trick, leaving some large deposits for whoever wants to clean the sink. The smell bought me back to life. I picked up my cash and phone and got out as quick as I could. Though I was all over the place and doing everything I could not to fall over Hopefully I would have at least fifteen minutes start on the bad boys and girls. I rang a taxi based in Barmouth and they said they would be me in ten. They always do. I added some urgency and agreed to meet on the main road. There was no one about as I passed the pub and crossed the railway line. I ended up sitting amongst the long grass and trees on the other side of the main road. Hopefully out of sight.

Why is it when I find the right woman, she turns out to be the wrong one. This one did it in less than three days. The drugs may have affected me, but large doses of sorrow and self-pity were making a bigger impact. I really liked Ash and I thought she liked me, but I was just another job to her. When I bumped into her at the café it must have been staged. She stood behind me and ensured I walked straight into her with my tea. But how did she know I was in Prestatyn. I did not know I was going there myself and I made sure no one was following me. The clothes they provided in Birmingham; they may have had a tracker sewn in. Or the shoes I have on. Yes, the shoes. She had replacement clothes for me, but no footwear. They must have bugged the shoes.

Chapter Twenty-Four

The taxi arrived and I jumped in.

"Where's we off to?" said the chirpy driver.

"I'm heading to ether Llandudno or Chester."

"There's a bus leaves the island between Dolgleu and Barmouth for Llandudno, but its every two hours and take your pillow. There's a train from Blaenaeu to Llandudno, also we have a bus to Wrexham."

"How much to Llandudno?"

"If it's cash between you and me, no receipts, I'll do it for seventy quid and I'll even throw a coffee in."

"Sounds a lot of money," I said. "But I'll go for it. Need a quick stop to buy some clothes and shoes."

"No problem I'll make a detour to Porthmadog and I'll get the coffee whilst you are tarting yourself up."

The driver did a U-turn, and I threw my shoes into the undergrowth. He made a wise quip, saying he hoped I had showered. We passed the pub again – all was quiet.

I stonewalled attempts the driver made to strike up a conversation and tried hard to work out exactly what had happened. Whether it was the drugs or me realising that I had reached rock bottom I had become emotional, I was ready to cry. I felt betrayed and the only time in life I had felt like this was when I split with Angie. I was upset by a woman who I thought I would be spending time with over the next few months. But it was a lot more than another entry for my list of failed lovers. Ash and the Greek guy were working for a group of people killing young men. Well, I only knew about three men, there could have been women, older people, teenagers – who knows. The guys that were killed, did they deliver the bag or were they killed because they failed to complete their mission. It is all very well being on the run, but when you don't know who you are running from or why it is impossible to know where to hide. A list of places to head to ran through my mind. Ireland or Spain sounded good, maybe out of the way in some remote village in Scotland, but I'm not going to go far without cash, and I was running out of money. Gary Parsons is the man, if ever I needed a mate, it was now, I had to find him and pick up the wad. That would mean heading home, it was important I found him without being spotted. When I got to Llandudno I would give him a ring, we would meet up and I would survive for a couple of months with the lump of cash and maybe find some work along the way.

Chapter Twenty-Five

The journey to Porthmadoc was uneventful, driving through Harlech and catching some beautiful scenery along the way. We drove into the seaside town, there was a number of bus stops on the left and he pointed to an upmarket café on the right.

"We'll meet up there when you've got your stuff," he said, before dropping me in front of a clothes shop in the High Street.

There was a couple of clothes shops close to each other, so my socked feet did not see too much of the pavement. I bought two pairs of chinos, one beige, one blue and three cheap polo shirts, a hoody, boxers and socks. I found a discount chain shoe shop, common to most small towns. The trainers were cheap and looked like old stock from the 70s, so I bought brogue lookalike shoes.

On my way to the coffee shop headache tablets were purchased and I also stocked up on water. My head had pounded ever since I had been sick in the caravan. It was similar to the feeling I got when I was knocked out in Birmingham, though this time it was more like someone had crept inside my head with a bass drum and refused to stop banging it.

"You all right for ten minutes?" the driver said as I walked up to the counter at the café.

I nodded, ordered a drink and a sandwich before sitting down at a table big enough for four and took a couple of tablets before picking up my phone. I took the chance to ring Gary before we got to Llandudno. Gazer's phone rang out, I felt my heart beating throughout my body. It was all down to a new threat to panic about. The ringtone told me Gary was overseas. Had he taken my cash and gone on holiday? Not Gazzer, he wouldn't. We have been mates ever since we could walk. Where is he? He's got my cash, my passport and any real hopes of getting out of this mess. I unfolded the piece of paper Michelle had given me. Was she involved in the conspiracy or just another woman waiting to join the list of females who have kicked me when I was down? It is possible she was part of the plan? But Michelle had a regular job, and it was unlikely she was put on shift Monday to get to me. I had to trust someone, and I was running out of contenders. The question I asked myself about Michelle at Euston and repeated now was 'why me?' She is a stunner and appears sophisticated. Surely, she could do better than me. I put the doubts behind me and called her. It rang out – I left a message. That was that then. I decided to head to the Midlands, but would go via Liverpool or Manchester, just in case they thought I was heading home directly from Wales. There were two trains to Manchester every hour. One to Manchester Victoria with a change and a straight train to Manchester Piccadilly. The other also had two trains an hour with a change at Liverpool Central. I decided to head for Manchester and get the Megabus down to Birmingham which would save me some money.

The taxi driver walked towards me stocked with food, hot and cold drinks. "You ready?"

We walked a few yards to the car.

"Could you drop me at Llandudno Junction railway station?"

"That's easy for me," he replied. "You're doing some miles on the quiet?" I chose not to reply to his leading question, and he put the radio on.

"Nothing against Radio Wales mate, but I have got a head worse than an old grizzly who has drunk a barrel of Jack Daniels. Could you just play it in the front?"

He completed my request and remarked how miserable I was. I didn't reply and that brought a closure to any dialogue as I was asleep within two minutes.

My head jolted backwards. I was startled, it was only my phone and I must have been dreaming. I could swear we had crashed. Michelle was calling me back – I soon returned to my senses.

"I'm on my way to Birmingham, but I never learned where you lived. Wasn't sure if you were based in London or the Midlands. I was just looking to fulfil my promise. Do you fancy meeting up tonight?"

She laughed and said: "You don't mess about, do you?"

"You told me not to let you down."

"I live in Solihull, so Birmingham's not a problem."

"No. I'll see you in Solihull – I'll wait at the Centre at 7:30."

I was not too familiar with Solihull, so suggested a pub five minutes from the smaller of the towns two shopping centres, which I had visited with Angie in my domesticated days. We had been out looking at furnishings and other stuff we could not afford.

"We're like a pair of teenagers on our first date. I'll see you in O'Neill's.

That call lifted my spirits, and the sleep took away the severe headache. I was left with just a light, muzzy head. A huge improvement.

"How much further driver?"

"Nearly there pal."

"Looks like I've got a wait for my train. Is there a coffee shop nearby?"

"I'll drop you at the supermarket, they've got a café and it's only two- or three minutes' walk from the station."

Chapter Twenty-Six

As I walked towards the entrance of the supermarket, out of the corner of my eye I spotted a refrigerated van with a Birmingham telephone number. The driver was listening to the radio and eating his dinner.

"Sorry to disturb you. You heading back to Brum mate?"

"Yea, Washwood Heath."

"Any chance of a lift?'

"Dunno mate – we ain't supposed to take passengers."

"You'd be doing me a big favour and I'll give you £20."

"Alright. I'm going in ten."

"Fine. I'll go to the toilet and get a coffee – want one?

"Arr – two sugars mate, but don't pee in it. It tastes bad enough as it is."

Everyone's a comedian. I was back in five and handed the driver his coffee. We introduced ourselves.

"So, where are you heading?"

"I'm going to Mell Square.

"Paul, it's your lucky day. I live in Solihull. You will have to jump out before I get to the yard, but I'll pick you up and take you when I've handed over and sorted tomorrows work out."

We spent half an hour talking about football. As an Albion fan I was alright in Decker's eyes. He was Birmingham City, and we shared a common dislike of the 'big club' in the area. Decker must have given a good 15 minutes of his time to his boyhood hero, Trevor Francis, who I had only seen in old clips or as a pundit on TV.

"You look like you've been on the beer non-stop for a fortnight – your eyes are lifeless. Take a nap son – I won't mind as long as you don't snore your head off."

I woke up just as we were getting into Birmingham. My muscles ached and I still felt tired, though I had another deep sleep undisturbed by the noisy truck or Deckers non-stop sounds from the 80s that were now ringing in my ears. He turned his music down and looked over the cab at me.

"Back in the land of the living then our kid? You needed that didn't yer? Look. There's a McDonald's about five or ten minutes from the yard. I'll drop you there and pick you up half hour later."

"Do you want me to get you anything?"

"Nah, you're joking aren't yer. The missus is doing chicken breasts and tomatoes wrapped in bacon and mozzarella cheese. Her signature dish. You can keep yer nuggets and fries. See you in a bit – fill yer boots our kid."

I devoured the burger and fries; all I had eaten today was a sandwich in Porthmadog as breakfast did not go to plan. Two bottles of water were soon emptied to satisfy my raging thirst and a coffee to perk me up as I was flagging. Decker dropped me off an hour and a half before Michelle was due to arrive. The offer of an extra five pounds was refused - he told me I would need it.

"She must be some sort of special lady – have yourself a good night."

"Thanks Decker, you've been a god send."

Chapter Twenty-Seven

The thought of ringing Michelle and asking her to make her way to the pub early was soon dismissed. I would get a couple of pints down my neck before she arrives. The pub was one of those large mock Tudor buildings and was now part of a chain. Not a typical Irish pub or bar, more Irish themed. They played an Irish tune every so often and it had an Irish feel to it, but was a long way from the bars of Ireland or the Irish pubs scattered round the globe. One good thing, I knew I would get a decent pint of Guinness.

Within five minutes of sitting down my first pint was demolished. The second did not take much longer. It was going down far too easily this evening, but I needed the black stuff to relax. I convinced myself the iron would do me good and would help the nerves before my big date. I dare not think what would happen if it went wrong tonight.

Michelle walked in. Her hair was down, and she was dressed casually in jeans and a thin sweater but looked even better than she did in uniform on Monday. I am not sure if it was relief I was experiencing when she turned up or the sheer satisfaction that she had walked into this pub to see me. A huge grin had taken over my face and attempts at being cool had failed. We hugged, before staring at each other from close range, followed by an embarrassing silent moment.

"So, what are we drinking then?"

"I'll just take a coffee to get me started please."

Standing at the bar waiting for another pint, my mind began to wander. In fact, it was lost in the valley of confusion. I felt so good meeting Michelle – I can't remember feeling like this before. But at the back of my head, questions were bouncing off the inside of my skull like a pinball machine. 'Who is she?' 'Why me?' Why has it ended up so well today? I started the day being poisoned by a woman who I thought had feelings for me, escaped like a fugitive and ended up with a pint of Guinness and a date I could have only dreamt about a week or two ago. Unfortunately, I also asked myself the question: 'Is she just the next Aislinn, waiting to poison me?' As I took a sip from my glass before carrying the drinks to our table, I told myself I must forget all that stuff. Michelle is the real deal. She told me about her day, without moaning. I started telling her what had gone on since we met on the train.

"It's obviously distressing," she said. "It will keep."

We talked about our love lives, homes, likes, and dislikes. Michelle had moved to Solihull with her boyfriend of two-years. She spent a further two-years with him in their flat, before he decided he wanted more out of life and headed to Australia. Her parents and most of her friends still lived in Bromsgrove, around 20 miles away. Michelle visited the town on the outskirts of Birmingham at least once a week and was thinking about moving back there.

I had another pint and we talked with each other like old friends. What she had done, what she wanted to do. She was transparent, answered every question whether it was negative or positive. I had turned into a relentless old reporter, trying to find every grain of information. She did not tell to stop, but I realised what I was doing and cooled off.

Michelle suggested we go to a bar about five minutes' walk away. As we went up the road, she grabbed my hand, and we took a deep look into each other's eyes. I felt so good. The next stop was more food and cocktails. Plenty of couples eating and drinking, but I would imagine it to be a party zone Friday and Saturday. Again, I asked Michelle if she wanted to eat, but she politely declined. I insisted she started on the cocktails and was pleasantly surprised when I was served a decent pint of Guinness. We talked about football, music, going out and both gave brief family histories, avoiding my imminent danger. I hardly knew this woman, but the more we talked the closer we got – I hadn't met anyone like her. She was on my wavelength – I was talking to my dream woman. I told myself: 'Don't blow it Paul.'

I stood up to fetch another drink, possibly our last, then Michelle asked me to sit down.

"Look I'll get the drinks in," she said. "You have got a lot on, and it is obvious it is worrying you. Whatever is going on, it has no effect on me. I really like you. Even though it is early days.

"Stay at mine. I'm back early tomorrow and we will have a chat then. I don't want you to stress tonight. I need you cool and calm."

I grinned and nodded. Michelle headed for the bar.

She returned with my Guinness and her 'Dark 'n Stormy' - rum with ginger beer and lime. "You like your rum then?"

"Yea. I went out to the Caribbean on holiday – it was less than half price thanks to my job. Loved the beaches, loved the food, loved the people and guess what? The rum was good too."

I laughed and a dream entered my head of us two walking across the beach in Tobago or some other exotic island. Typical of me. Dreaming. Two steps ahead of the game and often missing out what's happening in the present. More like a whole street ahead this time. Get real Paul. We finished our drinks after a short trip around the world, talking about some of the places we had visited.

"Right. Mine's only ten minutes from here. Hope you have your pyjamas in that carrier bag," she said with her infectious laugh.

Chapter Twenty-Eight

Michelle lived in a block of around a dozen nice apartments, and she had decorated it quite distinctively. Though she was easy going and a fun person to be with, I also got the impression that this was a lady who knew what she wanted in life.

"I've got just the one bedroom. I'll be waiting for you if you want to shower or wash. The bathroom is over there."

Taking a glance in the steamed-up mirror of the bathroom cabinet I asked myself if I was dreaming. No. I t was so much better than a dream hearing Michelle laugh, smelling her perfume, listening intently to her every word. How I got here, I'll probably never know. What happens next? Who cares.

I walked into the bedroom with a towel round me. The lights were off, Michelle was lying on her side facing me. Her left hand supporting her face with her elbow in the pillow. I stood there contemplating my next move.

"You going to stand there all night?"

I settled into the huge bed, and she leaned over and gave me a long lingering kiss.

Chapter Twenty-Nine

At just after 11am I woke up following one of my best night's sleep for a very long time. I probably slept with a huge grin on my face – I woke up smirking with a buzz running through my veins. It was unreal knowing I had woken up in Michelle's bed. After showering and putting on fresh clothes purchased in Porthmadog I walked into the kitchen and picked up a note.

I read it out loud: "Just switch the percolator on and coffee will magically appear in five minutes. Milk, bacon and sausage in fridge. Bread, and eggs on side. Sugar in cupboard above percolator. Had a great night. "I took a long breath before continuing. "Don't run off. I need you and I want you. Michelle. Kiss, kiss, kiss."

My grin reached both ears and I stood in the kitchen for at least 30 seconds before fixing breakfast. I sat down in front of the TV with a bacon and egg sandwich and a mug of coffee. I can understand why so many of those folks who must stay at home go crazy. Daytime TV should shoulder most of the blame. It is all so negative or fake. I ended up watching an all-day news channel, though that turned out to be the same old stories repeated every hour.

There was an outline of a plan in my head, but it was not impressive. I needed money and had to see if my best mate had run off with the cash. His dad and my dad would be having a pint and a game of crib tomorrow lunchtime, so that's where I would be heading.

The landline rang.

It was Michelle: "I bet you thought shall I answer that?"

"I did wonder."

I heard a giggle at the end of the phone before she replied: "Look Paul, I am on my way, and I thought we would get a pizza for tea. I'll be there in an hour – what do you want?"

My simple requests were noted, and I was close to telling her how good she was but thought that was over the top – even for me. I felt a teenager waiting for her to come home, though she could cool off once I have told her the full story. In this short time, I had a higher regard for Michelle than I had for any other woman I had met, but I had to tell her everything. I would start as I meant to go on. No lies. No glossing over the negatives.

Chapter Thirty

We ate our pizzas and I turned down offers of beer and wine. As soon as I had digested the last mouthful, I told Michelle everything. My relationship with Angie, life on the breadline since our split, my dinghy flat in a town I didn't want to live in before detailing where I had been since finding the package and the fear that someone was out to get me and has possibly killed three guys of a similar age to me in London. Michelle did not interrupt me and let me explain in full.

"Right, I think it's time we had that drink," she said, standing up and making her way to the kitchen.

She returned with two bottles of beer.

"All this hasn't put me off," she said. "You are in a mess and a right mess – I can't see a quick way out. But now's not the time to abandon you. In this short time, I have grown to like you too much. You never know, we might make a good couple, but that's the last of our worries."

"I did wonder if you would send me packing or maybe not believe me."

She laughed and answered: "I don't think anyone could make a story like that up. If you could, you'd be writing best sellers. What's your plan, then?"

"Well, money makes the world go round and mines running out fast. Gary's got ten grand of mine, well cash I've claimed. His dad will be having a pint with my dad down the club tomorrow dinner – I'll be heading to Halesowen and see if Charlie knows where he is."

"That's a good start, but you still need to get these people off your back. Be nice to know what they want. I'm starting at New Street tomorrow, not too early. Do you want to come in with me and get a breakfast up town to wind away an hour or so before seeing your dad?"

"Yea that would be great. No bus into town just the bus back home."

"We'll meet later."

Michelle took a long hard look at me and said: "Now's not the time to feel sorry for yourself. Life's been crap for a while. You need to find Gary – don't keep thinking the worst. Then you need to sort these people out. I don't think you can do it on your own and do you really want to carry on being on the run from people you don't know or even know what they look like or what they want?"

I did believe the worst-case scenario with Gazzer, but she was right I needed to be positive. A night with Michelle twinned with this mess was still better than a poor job and a miserable bedsit in Kidderminster. Michelle took the bottle of beer out of my hand and put it on the table with hers. She then pulled me towards her and gave me the tightest of hugs – like she never wanted to let me go.

"Soon we will be rid of all this and be really happy," I said.

"I am really happy," she replied before placing a solitary upright figure against her lips somehow snuggling up even closer. I do not think she was telling lies when she said she was happy – it was her belief that everything would be rosy in the future that I struggled with.

Chapter Thirty-One

I walked up to Colmore Row in Birmingham near the station I used to catch the train from when I worked at White Beam. After resisting the temptation to revisit room 14 of the Beaumont Hotel I jumped on the number nine bus. In my mind I was convinced a trip to the hotel would be futile as Zorba and any of his colleagues would be long gone.

Sitting upstairs on the bus travelling out of the city, I was surprised that I felt glad to be back in Birmingham and felt like I missed it. It was the place where I went to college and I had some of my best night outs in the Second City, but never thought I would miss it.

When the bus rolled into the station in Halesowen, I was running early so I decided to kill half an hour with a walk around what we used to call the Precinct as kids and grab another coffee. After finishing my newspaper, I headed towards the club.

On opening the door, I smelt the familiar odour of disinfectant from the stone floors of the passageways. Memories flooded back of Christmas parties when we all got decent toys and Saturday mornings when I used to accompany my dad and drink pop whilst he sorted some club work out. The bar now had carpet so a few members could play indoor bowls.

"How am yer dad?"

"Alright son – not heard from you lately. Your mum's starting to worry." "Tell her I'm fine – I'll ring her later."

"OK. No bullshit son – you best ring her today."

"How am yer Charlie?"

Good Paul., better than the Baggies, that's for sure."

"I've been trying to get hold of Gazzer, but it sounds like he's abroad."

"Nah – he's got two phones. Gave one to one of his blokes, whose phone died, but needed a mobile on holiday. He's still got his work phone. Hey – I'll ring him now."

Charlie passed me his old phone, I borrowed a pen and copied the number onto a beer mat and walked out to the corridor to ring him.

"Did you think I'd done a runner," Gazzer chuckled.

"Well, I had my doubts."

"I know what you want mate, I'll finish here, pop home and come to you." "How about if we meet at the Queens Head in an hour?"

"Sound. See you then. Mine's a cider."

Chapter Thirty-Two

As I have done ever since I can remember, I stood on the pavement and looked left and right preparing to cross the road. There was a gap then, whatever happened next, I have no knowledge of. I awoke with Zorba's hands around my neck, his face was screwed up concentrating on killing me off. A woman screamed and Zorba removed his hands and disappeared. I looked around. I was in a hospital bed. Four people attended to me before I was left with a middle-aged nurse.

"You were in a road traffic incident," she explained.

"When?"

"Yesterday. You have been out cold. The doctors will be with you shortly. You are a lucky man. Patients who are out cold don't always come back alert like you."

"You know. Being in a road accident that I can't remember followed by a big bloke trying to take my last breath of not so fresh air doesn't seem so lucky to me."

"Mr Ellis, I can assure you, that you were lucky on both counts."

"I'm parched, can I get a cup of tea nurse?"

"Not yet. You best wait for the doctors."

Not one, but two doctors, gave me a thorough examination.

The older doctor who peered down his nose over his glasses in a superior way, that comes naturally to only a few men in chosen professions, spoke to me.

"From our initial findings you appear to have returned from your coma in relatively good health. It is early days though and many more tests are required. We were surprised to find your blood pressure normal after the coma. We need to find out if there are any haemorrhages or even a weak spot in a blood vessel of the brain as well as looking out for abnormal clusters of blood vessels and tumours.

"I can't believe you didn't break your legs. The right leg is really battered, and it looks like your left arm is not too good.'

"Oh well, it is nice to know it is only my leg that is battered – got a few chips to go with it?" I quipped sarcastically.

"We will try and get you into surgery this afternoon."

"For what?"

"Mr Ellis, we started with an X-ray when you first arrived and found metal at the back of your neck."

"That's news to me."

"There would not be any medical reason to place a metal plate there and unfortunately that piece of metal also prevents other tests being made."

"Hopefully we will be able to do an MRI tomorrow and start working out to see if there has been any damage made to your head in what can only be described as a serious collision."

The pair left and a different voice boomed from the doorway: "Do you ever do anything, but doss about?"

"Michelle, how did you know I was here?"

"My number was in your pocket. I think you had written Goddess next to it. The hospital contacted me, and I have been here all the time you have been dead to the world. I even tickled between your toes, but no response."

"Your dad got here pretty quickly because you were knocked over outside his club.

"Your mum and dad have been beside themselves. They have just popped home – I'll ring them in a minute."

Chapter Thirty-Three

Two men in shirts, ties and suits were led into the small room I woke up in. "Thank you, nurse.

"Hello, I am Detective Inspector Brass and this is Detective Sergeant Chopra. "Madam, are you related to Mr Ellis?"

"No."

"Is it possible that you could wait outside or in the cafeteria whilst we ask Mr Ellis a few questions?"

"I'm Paul and anything you have to say you can say in front of Michelle." "Don't make a fuss Paul – it's not a problem."

"Thank you, madam. Your name is?"

"Michelle Fagan."

"Are you in a relationship with Paul?"

"I am and I'm proud of it," she said with a big grin and a wink to me as she walked away. "Can you recall being knocked over on Hagley Road, Halesowen?"

"No. I remember standing at the side of the road. Next thing I'm in here."

"You weren't knocked down as you crossed the road. A white Ford Transit mounted the pavement and deliberately drove at you. We are treating it as attempted murder. Do you know of anyone who would try to kill you in broad daylight?"

"No."

"Earlier today a man tried to kill you in this room. He was thick set muscular man with short dark hair. Do you know him?"

"No."

"Come on. One attempted murder could be coincidence, but another the following day is careless Mr Ellis".

"Think about those two situations. Can you give me the slightest morsel of information to help my enquires. And to make sure we don't get a third attempt on your life."

Detective Sergeant Chopra then added his view: "They have tried twice – I can't see them giving up. You need to tell us everything. All we have at the moment is the assailant was driving a white Transit, no registration to go on and a poor description of what appears to be hired muscle trying to kill you in your hospital bed. He didn't speak so we haven't a clue where he came from. We need your help Mr Ellis, and you need us to put these fellas away before they succeed in killing you."

"You haven't been to work in over a week. What's going on?"

"If you have been in touch with White Beam, they would tell you they were about to sack me for poor sales figures."

"You've got a bit of an attitude," Detective Inspector Brass responded. "As Detective Sergeant Chopra has told you, you need us if you want to stay alive – so start cooperating. What have you been doing since leaving your employers?"

"Not a lot. Took a ride out on the train and spent a few days at my girlfriend's flat." "Has anybody tried to assault you or threaten you?"

"No officer. I've never been in trouble in my life."

"Yes, we checked you out. Just because you have never been caught doesn't mean you have not been involved in criminal activities. I would say that the people involved with these two attempted murders are hardened criminals – you've upset someone, somewhere."

They continued gathering what appeared to be insignificant details before telling me I would be moving rooms and an officer would be permanently positioned outside the door. The pair left and before Michelle had time to pop in, they wheeled me off to surgery.

Chapter Thirty-Four

Mum, dad and Michelle were waiting for me in my new room. As promised by Detective Inspector Brass a police officer was now shadowing my every move. I asked a nurse for water, tea and dinner. The first two were delivered and was told I wouldn't have to wait too long for food.

"We just wanted to see you were alright Paul," said Mum. "They said you could be tired so we will leave you with Michelle and head home. We'll be back tomorrow."

"Glad to see you are alright. You've got a good 'un there," Dad added, nodding at Michelle. "You best stop running around and grow-up now a decent woman wants you."

I could have done without all that, but he did not mean any harm.

Michelle waited for them to leave before saying: "I'm a good un – you've got to look after me."

Her tone changed: "Right. I have hardly spoke to you in days. You best tell me what the coppers have said and why they wheeled you off to surgery."

"I had surgery because they reckon I have metal in the back of my neck and they need to do scans on my head and can't do it whilst I had this metal there."

"Did you have an operation of metal splinters from an accident or something?" "Never."

Neither of us seemed too concerned, just startled finding out about it. "How about the coppers?"

"They reckon I am up against professional criminals. The one was pushing me as though I was a criminal. He says just because I haven't got a record doesn't mean to say I'm not a villain.

"The Transit that run me over definitely was out to get me. He drove onto the pavement. Also, I was in a coma, but that big Greek wrestler type bloke I told you about from the Birmingham hotel was trying to strangle me when I was in a coma. I woke, but I doubt if I could have stopped him, luckily a nurse screamed at him. The coppers know something big is going on, to have two attempted murders on the same bloke on consecutive days. That's why there is a Rozzer outside the door, and we have to be careful what he hears."

"Life has been pretty calm apart from that then," she quipped.

I just smiled.

"Look you are going to have to get the police involved. Tell them everything."

"I can't trust them to get the job done. They would only attract attention and make it easier for this faceless gang to find me. Wish I knew what they wanted. Did they get what they wanted from those three and then killed them or do they kill everyone that they give a job to?"

"You will be on the run for a long time or dead Paul – don't try and be a hero."

We chatted for a while, but you could tell she wasn't pleased with me. Michelle was really worried about me. She had gone pale, lost some of her exuberance and started avoiding my gaze and looked at the floor.

Michelle kissed me and promised to visit tomorrow in the afternoon or evening. She walked to the end of the bed and took a long look at me, her eyes started welling up and she made a hasty exit.

Chapter Thirty-Five

A doctor and a group of trainees came in to see me at 9am the next morning. They spoke about my legs and said I would be getting occupational therapy and the use of an aid to walking. I presume he meant crutches. The last thing my street cred needs is a walking frame. They fobbed me off when I asked about the metal at the back of my neck. 'We will be discussing that later' was the stock answer.

Half an hour after the doctors left an extremely good-looking honey blond nurse walked into my room. She was flirty, which surprised me.

"So, what did the doctor say this morning?"

"Nothing new. They will arrange some occupational therapy and an aid to walking. I can't have a walking frame – just think of my street cred."

She laughed.

"So, it sounds like they are ready to pack you off. Where will you go? Do you live on your own?"

"I don't know yet. Haven't thought about it. My place is not too good with a broken leg."

"You are welcome round mine Hun. And if not, we are going to have to have a night out or a night in together Paul."

I was flattered and loved the attention she was giving me. I could not get over how direct this woman was. She really wanted me, yet we had only just met. Something is not right here.

"So, I know you are very attractive and for some reason you want a night out with ugly old me. I don't know what your name is."

She showed me her name tag and said: "Rachael McDonald, as in Big Mac, large fries and a shake. Let's have a look at your legs."

The nurse had a quick look at the plastered bottom half of the one leg and then used both hands to rub the other leg.

"Nice legs."

She then rubbed both my legs at the same time, gently. I was telling myself I only want Michelle and then looked away in embarrassment as I was aroused - it would have been evident to Rachael.

"Hey Paul. I think you like that."

A smile appeared on her face, she stood up and put the sheet back over me.

"I'm on a long day today. I'll pop back before visiting around three, the results will have been typed up then. Hopefully you will be on your own and I get you all to myself again."

Chapter Thirty-Six

At 2pm, two smartly dressed men in their mid-forties joined me. One with hair, Les Carter the other without, Eric Reeve. I guessed they were from Special Branch or similar, I was unlikely to be told. They just gave me their names: I knew immediately they were not messing about.

The bald officer stood close to the bed and spoke softly: "This is an extremely serious situation; you are involved in Paul. We would not be here if it wasn't. We don't do hit and runs."

"It is important you cooperate with us," Carter added. "If you have gained financially or dipped your toe in criminal activities, it doesn't matter. We are looking at the situation overall. Do you wish to cooperate?"

"I will. And there is one thing I need to say before we go any further. A nurse came to me this morning. Rachael McDonald was the name she gave - extremely attractive. Blonde shoulder length hair, skinny model frame around 5' 7" in height. I don't think she's a nurse. She's coming back at three."

They both looked at their watches simultaneously and Carter spoke: "Right, we will leave it there for the moment and come back to you soon."

The pair didn't go to the local nurse's station but made their way to the main administration office. The only MacDonald's they had on the system was Rose who had recently retired and a doctor by the name of Peter. Rachael was not listed. Whichever way you spell it.

They returned to the wards, one dressed as an orderly. The other a doctor. The officer babysitting would contact the pair by radio, without speaking as soon as she arrived.

Reeve and Carter watched as the woman dressed as a nurse went into my room. A listening device was planted earlier, and the pair waited. She walked in with a coffee in a takeaway cup along with a soft drink and straw.

"How are you feeling?"

"Yea. Good."

"Let's have a look at those legs of yours. I hope the staff have been looking after them for me."

She gently caressed my thighs.

"Here you are?" she said handing over the soft drink. "Drink this whilst I concentrate on making you relaxed."

The two officers burst in.

"Don't drink it Paul," said Reeve.

A call was put out for officers to collect the fake nurse.

The officer then grabbed Rachael's left arm and questioned her: "I believe the drink will turn out to be poisoned, what was in it?"

"Don't know it was given to me," Rachael replied

Two officers came to collect her, and Reeve gave instructions: "Bang her up for a few hours. We'll speak to her later and start with attempted murder."

The woman turned ashen and shook her head.

"Let's get back to our conversation," said Reeve. "So how did you get involved?" I gave the two detectives the full story from the moment I found the package. "Have you ever seen the Greek guy before?" asked Carter.

"No. The first time I saw him I was coming round from being knocked out."

"All through this sorry episode, you have not seen anyone you have ever met before or connections to work or friends?"

"No."

"The Irish woman in Wales would have been tipped off in with a call from London. That tracker told them where you were going. We will have a look round the area, but I reckon she will be long gone. If not like Rachael, there will be very little she can tell us. They are both small fish."

I knew these guys would want more from me and I would be the one risking my life. There appeared to be a good chance someone would kill me within a month or if I could get away I would spend the rest of my life on the run on my own hoping they will not get to Michelle. Hopefully I could cut a deal with these pair.

Reeve addressed me from the bottom of the bed as Carter sat in the chair.

"Right Paul. We can see you have had a right old game, and this matter is far from finished. We can sort some protection out. Live wherever or go back to work, but we are dealing with top international criminals, who kill at the blink of an eye. Invariably they are going to find you and the 24/7 protection we can provide will be challenged sooner rather than later.

Reeve takes a deep breath, looks at his partner and looks back at me before continuing. "Alternatively, you can help us nail them."

"International villains, not scared to murder, three attempts on my life already – what's a telesales bloke going to do?"

"They want you for some reason. They are going to come after you – it is best if we work together."

"Yea, but you have admitted your security is not good enough."

"I said if you lead a normal life with our operatives shadowing you, they will get you in the end. I am proposing a period of up to six-weeks where three times that number will be supporting you.

"Tell me more."

"You will need to be here for a couple of days and then I'm giving you four or five-days break before we get to work, and you entice the big boys into play. They want you, we have a few ideas who they are, why they want you is another thing. You will be brought up to speed after your break, when you get to hobble a bit quicker."

"OK I can see where you are coming from. I have a few demands."

The pair nodded in unison.

"Michelle comes with me. You move all her stuff out of her flat into storage. For all intense and purposes – she has vanished. If after six weeks we find some baddies,

but there are plenty of others taking their places, we both need new identities with a financial settlement."

Reeve responded: "Yea OK. I need to get clearance for the new identity and settlement. I will make the call shortly and if all is well getting some paperwork together tomorrow."

I was shocked that they could move things along so quickly. I genuinely did not know who wanted me dead, but I was surprised the Special Branch did not dig deeper for further details. How did they know I was telling the truth? It all seemed too cozy.

Chapter Thirty-Seven

At 4pm Michelle walked in with immaculate hair and make-up along with freshly painted nails. Her makeover did not extend to the worried look and frown that has become permanent.

"Hi Ya Babe"

"You look a million dollars."

She forced a smile.

"And it's all for you. What's happening – any medical news or have the coppers rounded them up."

"Nah – but I have had a few visitors. Two Spooks came today and a mysterious woman." "Spooks?"

"Yea. Intelligence services, MI5, Special Branch or whatever. Anyway, I have had a couple of visits from a nurse who wanted to rub my legs, she said I had lovely legs and was really worried about where I was going when I was discharged. Wanted me to go back to hers or at least go on a date."

"Did she have a white stick and a dog?"

"Definitely not. She had the looks of a model and she wanted me, but I had to turn her down because I met this dark-haired woman „who wasn't too bad and makes a decent bacon sarnie."

"You mean she put her glasses on and ran off?"

"Seriously, something happened. I was suspicious and told the Spooks. When she came back at 3pm she had a drink for me, that was poison."

Michelle's jaw dropped.

"She's been arrested. Though the Spooks reckon she won't know a lot." "This isn't funny Paul. That's three attempts to kill you."

"I had a chat with these two guys, and they propose I help them catch the guys who are after me. Take a break for a few days then sort it out."

"So, are you going to be a sitting target then? What's the alternative?"

"Go on the run, for a long, long time or try and lead a normal life with some protection that won't be good enough."

"What did you say?"

"I said I would cooperate but made some demands. I said I wanted you to come with me – that's if you agree. They move all your stuff out of the flat into storage and if after six weeks it's still going on, we'll both need new identities and a financial settlement. Do you want to dodge bullets with a fugitive?"

"I couldn't think of a better fugitive to dodge bullets with," she said with a genuine smile.

"They are going to give me something in writing tomorrow, they are running it passed their bosses now. If it all adds up, I will need a day or two here before we go on a break for four or five days. Might have a stick or something to help me walk."

"I'll see if I can get you a parrot, Long John Silver. Whatever happens I've made the right decision. I would sooner be with you and dead in a fortnight than you get hunted down on your own."

Those words of commitment and affection hit home. Not only does she love me, but she's also prepared to lose everything. It made me feel good, but I can't let it her be harmed. Michelle put her head on my chest, tears streamed down her cheeks as I stroked her hair. We were silent – speech would be a distraction and we remained silent for around two minutes.

A nurse walked in, and Michelle stood up.

"No worries. I'm just having a quick look at his leg and taking a few bloods. You can stay here," said the nurse.

"It's okay, I'm off to the washroom," said Michelle whose eyes were still full of tears.

Michelle returned to the side ward, just as the nurse was packing up and getting ready to leave.

"He's quickly healing my love. I'll get a stick for him and see if we can get the physiotherapy people to start later. We should have your bloods back today."

Whilst out Michelle re-applied her make-up and there were no signs that she had been crying. She gave me a hug but pulled away.

"I don't want to start crying again. We need to get ready to move on. I best get home."

"The two spooks will be here in half-hour. You best wait and speak to them. Not sure if it is good for you to go home, especially on your own. They are not going to tell us everything, but you can ask them a few questions."

"By the way, two big blokes are now outside guarding you."

I smiled, though I doubt it was too convincing.

"Paul, I want to settle down when all this is over. I think you do too. Where do you want to go?"

"Well, if there is still a danger or even if there is not, I fancy a new start. I would miss my mates and me mum and dad, but I would like to get away. I fancy the coast or somewhere hot – how about you?"

"Yea. Somewhere hot sounds good, but if everything ends up good in the next six weeks or so, we will need to work. I could sell the flat or rent it out – they are fetching decent money in Solihull."

"And I will give Gazzer a ring before the spooks get here – make sure he sorts the cash."

"Alright Paul. I trust you. I can't say that about too many blokes. I need you to promise me we will always talk our problems through. We are going to come up with all sorts of shit, but we need to stay together. No being the hero, no sulking or keeping stuff to yourself."

"You have no problems on that front – you're everything to me."

Michelle walked over and wrapped her arms round me. Her eyes filled up again, but no tears this time.

"Do you want to borrow my phone to call Gary?"

I dialled his number. Fortunately, no strange ring tone this time.

"Gary Monk."

"Hi Ya Gazzer. How's it going? Look I can't speak for long. You got the cash, passport and chequebook?"

"Yes mate. I was bringing it to you, but you weren't there. Only heard this morning you were almost killed outside the club. Though looking at my phone I reckon I got a missed call from the hospital two days ago."

"I'm alright now mate. Just need another big favour."

"Just say the word, Paul."

"I can't get the cash off you and if you pay it into my account, they probably won't accept it. I want you to go to one of the casinos on the Hagley Road and turn it all into chips. Play a couple of games and the cash the chips in and ask them to write you a cheque and pay it into your account. I'll let you know who to pay it to later.

"Didn't realise you were such a rogue?" Michelle questioned with a smile. "Nah. Just worked for a few dodgy people."

"So where would you like to live?"

"I think Spain, Italy, Greece or the Greek Isles. Somewhere you get the sun and we could live comfortably without spending a fortune. We will also need the option of getting back easily enough if we have to."

"Yea. I would be happy in the Greek Isles. Though unless we start an internet business, rent out a property or open a taverna, we won't have enough money for more than a few years."

"Let's wait and see if we are on the run in six weeks."

"Okay, but at the moment we must try and be happy and not take things too seriously. We've got a few days away. Let's see if I'm the best thing since sliced bread then."

Chapter Thirty-Eight

Reeve and Carter walked into the room. After the exchanging pleasantries, Carter talked about how the case was progressing.

"The very attractive nurse who wanted your body Paul, turned out to be a high-class hooker. It was just another job for her. Our Greek friend met her after he had made contact via the web. Told her to gain your confidence and give you the drink and make sure you drank it. That's all she knows. Never seen the Greek guy before and has no connections to this case. She did make a definite identification. Her photofit of the Greek guy and yours are almost identical."

'But it's a dead end,' I said.

"Afraid so, though we have another avenue to explore – we have a local cop who thinks he knows the giant. We have also followed a paper trail for payments made on the hotel in Birmingham. The same company has been paying it for 18-months, but they sub-let it for the last three-months. It is a long shot, but we are getting closer

there and we have a tie to the London hotel which seems careless. But as you say, the hooker is a dead end and we have not made any further arrests. One of our prime concerns is getting you better and making sure you are safe these next few days. We want you both to relax and hopefully spoil yourselves before Paul gets to work."

"What exactly will Paul be doing?" Michelle said firmly.

Reeve decided to take questions: "We don't know yet – depends on the info we get over the next few days. It is best you don't know anyway."

"So when do we leave?"

"Well, if all goes well with the physio this afternoon, we will leave between five and eight. If not, we will probably see more medics tomorrow."

"So shall I go and get my stuff and make sure I'm back for five."

"Sorry Michelle. You can't go home, and it could be a long time before you see your parents."

She looked at the detective dumbfounded.

"In about half-hour Vicki will speak to you on the phone. She is good. She will sort out new wardrobes, clothes that you like wearing, and have them ready for you when you get to the safe house this evening. Two of my men, will ensure your parents' house is safe, no one spying on them, and they will explain that you are fine, but can't speak to them at the moment. Vicki can also sort any medication or reading material you want along with all toiletries and perfumes. Paul will be treated the same. Michelle all your home contents will be stored safely and, in the future, can be delivered anywhere you want them without charge. If in the future, you need to sell or rent your property we can arrange that. Gary, your stuff will go in storage, and I am informing your landlord you are moving out as requested. Any other questions?'

I told Carter and Reeve there would be more questions at the end and asked if they expected it to go on for six weeks, but they were non-committal.

"Michelle, I need your keys, phone and your purse. Don't worry you will have another purse with cash and a card in it. During these next six weeks, you will not have your own phone and under no conditions are you to contact anyone. If there has been something you have forgotten and believe you need to contact someone, don't. Speak to one of the team. This is a big operation; other people will die if we fail."

Reeve took his mobile phone out of his jacket pocket, whilst Michelle handed over her personal possessions to Carter. Reeve rang Vicki and explained the situation before he handed over the phone to Michelle. She gave the operative a list of sizes, styles and brand preferences. She was even asked about perfume, makes of toothpaste and deodorant. I did the same. We were both given lunch from the trolley and there was a sense of unease between us.

The humour had gone and since the spooks departed, we had said little to one another. Michelle joined me and the physio as I was wheeled down the corridor with one of the spooks in close proximity.

Chapter Thirty-Nine

The physio, a mature woman in her fifties was assisted by a younger woman. They told me I would experience pain from my leg for a few weeks and to use painkillers when necessary. If new pains appeared from my arm, I would need to see a doctor. They gave me an elbow crutch that moulded into my arm and after a few steps walking became quite easy and without pain.

"Maybe in around a week, you will be able to dispense with the crutch, but keep hobbling about in the meantime – it will get easier." the physio said.

Back at the side ward Reeve told us the medication will be ready in 25 minutes and we would set off then. The meds arrived, I got into a wheelchair with my stick across my lap. Reeve pushed the chair, Michelle and the two spooks walked close by. We did not head to the entrance, but they wheeled me through a ward and opened the fire door at the end. Carter was waiting outside, a driver sat ready to go and the side doors of a Mercedes Multi-Purpose Vehicle were open. Reeve and Carter stayed behind, whilst Michelle and I sat on the back seat with a table in front of us. I felt like a celebrity with the blacked-out windows, though Michelle was not impressed. It might have something to do with the fact that we did not have a clue where we were going and who or why someone wanted me dead. Just over three hours after leaving the hospital we arrived at our destination. It was a hotel amongst a row of Edwardian three-storey houses. We climbed the half a dozen steps and a smartly dressed woman opened the heavy back door. We followed her into the house, and she introduced us as our host Jean. The interior was a surprise, deceptively large with five star trappings.

"I will let you settle in. How about dinner in 30 minutes?"

We both said thanks.

"Beef Stroganoff to your taste? Good. If you take the little lift round the corner, you are the first door on the right. Vicki dropped your clothes in earlier. I'm sure you will be comfortable here. It was a boutique hotel until we took over. There's only you and the lads staying here at the moment. If there is anything you need, just call me – I'm the other side of the landing to you. Take it easy tonight, watch TV, have a couple of drinks and Les and Eric will be round after breakfast."

The lift made life easier though my leg was not creating too much discomfort. The room, like the rest of the place was perfectly appointed. Every tapping of luxury. Michelle was impressed and she kicked off her shoes, pushed me onto the bed, before climbing on to the bed with her legs straddling me.

"Right Ellis. I've been waiting for this opportunity. You are going to suffer. I don't care about your leg."

"You are such a temptress. We just can't do this now. We have 25 minutes to shower, sort our stuff out and get downstairs. Then you have all night to have your wicked way with me."

"Okay. It really is going to happen – I'm going to sap whatever energy you had left in you."

Michelle laughed before kissing me gently. After a shower we looked at the clothes chosen for us. Not bad, good brands and not something my dad would wear. We walked across to the lift and got in. Michelle pushed me against the mirrored wall of the lift and kissed me forcibly.

"That's so you don't forget what's expected of you later."

We ate alone and were served a ten-year-old bottle of red wine to accompany a dinner fit for a top restaurant - not that I had been to too many lately.

"Okay man on the run, what we going to do when this matter is resolved," Michelle asked.

"Well, I thought we would do a John and Yoko, book into a hotel for a month, stay in bed and have room service for a month."

"Sounds good."

"Or move to some remote village near the sea or surrounded by countryside and knock a few kids out."

"You don't think either of us would want to work?"

"Mmmm. I thought about that. How about a bar on a Greek isle, in a village that's not too busy. Me and you, the dream team, running a taverna."

"So, you're into me now, are you?"

"Best thing that ever happened to me. Sorry it had to happen like this. But you have to take the good with the bad. Into you? Yea, the moment I laid eyes on you."

"So, I'm the best thing that ever happened to you? Well, you're... you can be okay." We both laughed.

As we were drinking our coffee, Carter came in.

"Everything to your satisfaction? Jean is a Corden Bleu chef and a great host.'

'Probably one of the best meals I've eaten,' I replied.

Michelle nodded.

'Well, you can take it easy for a couple of days. A doctor will pop in before dinner each day to take a look at your leg. Eric and me will meet up with you after breakfast tomorrow. Just five minutes – nothing important yet.'

The pair finished their coffees and Michelle savoured the last drops of a vintage brandy.

In the morning I followed Michelle into the bathroom and turned the shower on. Placing my right forefinger to my lips. She placed a hand around the back of my head and pulled me towards her whispering in my ear.

"Hey Paul, so you want to play in the shower, eh? I thought I drained you of your last ounce of energy last night."

I whispered in reply.

"You did. I feel like I fought 12 rounds in the boxing ring before getting knocked out with seconds to go."

Michelle smiled.

"I've put the shower on and I'm whispering as they have probably bugged the place." "You've watched too many James Bond films."

"Look if this goes wrong and we're on the run again, we'll need some cash. I haven't got credit cards or anything. You still got your purse with everything in it.'

She nodded.

"Okay. While we can roam, I'll get some phones and get Gazzer to transfer that money to your account."

"Won't they be following us?"

'Yea. Let me worry about that."

Michelle used two hands to pull my face to hers and gave me a long, sensuous kiss that left me feint headed and speechless. No one had ever made me feel like this. I hope it lasts.

"We will take it easy today, Do the tourist stuff and work out who's following us around. We will sort the phone out tomorrow."

Chapter Forty

Reeve and Carter sat at table for breakfast on the other side of the room. Michelle demolished her full English breakfast and I had that comfortably pleased feeling after eating smoked salmon and perfect poached eggs for the first time in years. The two Special Branch agents joined us after we had all finished eating.

"So, we have not formulated a plan yet," said Carter. "But I can assure you that you will be in danger and as such you are going to be the sprat that catches the mackerel. You pair are going to be hanging around here for around five days so make the best of it. Enjoy the food here and feel free to roam round the beach and town while we finalise the plans. You are in no danger here."

"Okay. How much danger are we going to be in? The other thing you said we would get some spending money and you would come up with a deal that we would be happy with."

Reeve joined the conversation.

'Look I don't think Michelle will be under any threat. She stays here until it is all over. You will be looked after. You won't get a fixed lump sum, but you will get a regular payment for the rest of your life – just like you are a government employee. Plus, there will be some money for setting up a new life and a new identity if that is what you want or need.'

He handed over a credit card.

"The cards pre-paid. There's a thousand pounds on it. I will come back to you tomorrow after breakfast with your offer. Have a think in the meantime where you want to start your new life together. It doesn't have to be Birmingham or Wolverhampton."

Reeve thought his comment was funny, chuckling to himself. A typical pompous southerner looking down his nose at anyone living north of Watford.

"Okay. We will work on our suntan today, have a chat and meet up tomorrow." "Enjoy. Don't forget the doc will look at you before dinner every night."

We rented deck chairs on the pebble beach close to the pier next to an old couple who were hard of hearing and insisted on shouting the most worthless observations at each other. After a walk on the old pier, we found a table outside a nice little coffee house. As we waited for our food, we started a conversation that we had been avoiding all morning.

"So where are we heading to? That's if you still want me tagging along?" "It's whether we you can put up with me."

"Keep working hard and flattering me – you might get the gig permanently."

"You know – I'd love to start a new life in the sun."

"Me too. But I'm a bit young to retire on the Costa Brava and join the old dears for games of bingo."

Michelle shook her head.

'Don't think we could retire just yet Paulie. We could open a bar. Neither of us mind working, we are chatty and would be good with the punters.'

"I'd give that a go. Me in my white shirt, black bow and waistcoat telling you what to do and making sure you do it post haste."

"Really? I'll be both the brain and the looks in the partnership – you will specialise in labouring. Doing exactly what I want, when I want."

Michelle gave me a knowing glance followed by a huge grin.

"Seriously it sounds like a plan. Find a lock-up bar, open only in the season and if we want, we could just do nights and spend days on the beach. But where?"

"You ever been to the Greek Isles?"

"Yea. I've been to Rhodes and Kos. Two of my best holidays. Loved it out there and I love the Greeks."

"When I was a kid, I went to Crete with mum and dad a couple of times. We had a Villa on a peninsular near the old capital. The beaches were brilliant, the bars were great and there weren't too many Brits. Definitely no bingo or kiss me quick hats. It would be ideal for us."

"Sounds good. We best see what Batman and Robin say tomorrow. Let's leave it there for a bit – you're going all gooey."

Michelle stood up came across the table to me and hugged me adding a kiss on the top of my head for good measure, before the waitress interrupted us with two plates of food.

I had that content feeling I had not felt for years. Not because of the gammon I had just eaten followed by my favourite syrup sponge pudding and custard. I was happy and I had got something to look forward to. Not feeling too energetic after the stomach busting lunch, we headed for Royal Pavilion Gardens and another deck chair, possibly twinned with reading our books or taking an afternoon nap. I settled into my deckchair, somehow satisfied with life. Big lunch, deckchair in a park in Brighton – what more could you ask for?

"You awake?"

"Like I've been snoozing."

"There was a lot of heavy breathing going on and you had your eyes shut for a long time." "So, what's the plan?"

'I see the doctor over the next few nights and get a clean bill of health. We see what Batman and Robin have to offer in the morning, but we will still go shopping, get some phones, and have Gaz transfer the money in case it all goes wrong. We won't get far on ten grand, but it would be a start and if we get you waitressing, I'm sure you will earn a few bob in tips."

The remark did not bring a smile to her face.

"It's not really a joke Michelle. It might work out like that. Us on the run taking low paid cash jobs to live. Do you really want that?"

"It wouldn't be my choice. But yes, I would do that. I would follow you to the moon and back Paulie."

"Oh no. The girl's going gooey again."

I took another look at a man in trousers and a formal shirt sitting to our left, he was totally out of place. He sat in a deckchair for around ten minutes after we got there and did not move.

She smiled this time and I believed what she told me. Where I went, she would follow, no matter what risk. I hope we would end up at a bar in Crete, but any planning for the future by me had come to a halt the moment Zorba decided I needed to rest for three days.

"Don't look now but I believe I have spotted our chaperone. He is on your left and looks more suited to the office than a deckchair. He has been sitting there. Not reading, playing with his phone, or snoozing. Has not eaten, drunk or even taken a pee. Let's get a pot of tea with a cake and see if he follows us."

Sitting in the window of a café with white tablecloths, the waitress presented our afternoon tea just as the man who must have been 50 years old walked past the window, crossed the road and sat at a bench in a position where he could look at us inconspicuously.

'Yea. He's, our man. Presume we get the same guy tomorrow. It makes it a bit easier – I know who I have to shake off when I get the phones.'

A middle-aged ex-military looking gentleman on our tail could not dampen my positive mood. I held Michelle's hand as we walked through the streets heading back to our room.

We showered and changed before making our way to a small lounge to wait for the doctor. The door swung open and a middle-aged tall man with a grey beard marched in.

He had an *it's only me who matters in life* look to him. Probably that superior god like attitude that many men in his profession also cultivate. He certainly did not dress like a top doctor in his jeans and creased button-down shirt.

"Michael Watkins. I'm here to have a look at you and check to see if the medics in Dudley have done their job."

I stood up. Lay down on the couch and stood up again with my shirt off. He prodded me. I sensed he got some sort of satisfaction dishing out pain.

"Are you taking the painkillers?"

"Haven't taken any today."

"Well, give it another three days and I don't believe you will get any further pain. By then you should get a clean bill of health. Try and keep off the painkillers and any other medication. If you must use them fine, but let me know. See you tomorrow. Same time, same place."

'Thanks Doc.'

We enjoyed another top notch three course meal and made use of the cheese board before the brandy and port arrived with our coffees. I must have drunk half a bottle of port. I was more than relaxed – happily drunk.

"You'll be good for nothing tonight. Let's get some sleep in," Michelle insisted. "We can explore Brighton's nightlife another evening."

Chapter Forty-One

The alarm went off at 8am, my head thundered, though it took me around 30 seconds sitting on the edge of the bed like a zombie to realise the port was pounding my brain. It was bad, but nothing like the pain Zorba's sedatives gave me on my unplanned stay in Birmingham. The thought of Zorba and his unknown accomplices brought me back to the real world after a day of bliss with Michelle. I walked to the bathroom and as the power shower pummelled the back of my neck, I considered how I would get phones whilst being trailed by our new friend and some money into Michelle's account. My thoughts moved to on to my meeting with Batman and Robin and concluded there would not be too much to think about until I received the offer and then it would be 'thank you very much' or 'what you are offering is not enough'. I like the idea of living in Crete, and once all this is over, I doubt it makes much difference to the government where I live. I should not kid myself. These are minor details. They have told me I will be the bait to catch the baddies – the big question is how, and will I survive?

Michelle turned over in bed and looked up at me.

"You might be clean and smell good, but you look like shit babe. Your eyes are lifeless. Cloudy like a murky pond."

"Morning Michelle. How are you on this glorious day? It is so nice to be alive and even nicer to be able to spend the day with you."

"Bullshit. The words might be flowing but I've seen livelier faces in the morgue, and you are walking about like a zombie. You best drink lots of coffee before the meeting, you alkie."

I did as I was told downing three cups of coffee as well as demolishing a full breakfast and four slices of toast. I was not at my best, but a lot better and ready to face the dynamic duo.

"You pair may as well stay at the table,' said Carter as Reeve put his cup on the table and sat down. "Okay lovebirds are you enjoying your stay? Being looked after?"

We both nodded. Not too interested in small talk, wondering what the offer would be.

"Okay guys this deal will be pretty simple. If everything goes to plan, we get the bad guys and you get to live a new life, whether you need one or not. We will pay you a monthly salary, not a lump sum, that will be index linked and increase annually with inflation. It will be like an average UK wage that you could live on if you pair don't get work. You will also get what we call moving costs to set you up in your new home. Whatever is needed for a new start. You won't get a lump sum but initially we will spend money setting you up. Now that's the good bit. If you die on this mission, Michelle won't get a widow's pension and there's no money for your family. As far as we are concerned, we didn't know you and there will be no connection to Special Branch. None whatsoever."

I looked over Michelle. Her face was blank.

Reeve decided it was his turn to talk.

"So kids, where do you want to go?"

"We've thought about it and fancy a new start. We are looking to open a bar on a Greek Isle. Is that possible?"

"Don't see why not. You have picked somewhere with reasonable living costs, and we have no beef with the Greeks."

Carter interjected.

"Any crucial questions about your new life?"

"Not really."

"Good. Give me another 48 hours and I'll sort a definite offer. I don't think we will have any problems."

"But you have not said what's happening. What do you want me to do?"

"We are not going to tell you until it happens. Will get the agreement sorted and off you'll go. Hopefully, you will come back to a new life, but as we said if you die – we never knew you."

"It all sounds precise – even clinical. With arrangements like this I can plan for a healthy retirement. That was sarcasm by the way - you guys don't care if I make my next birthday."

"So are you still up for it?"

I nodded unconvincingly.

Chapter Forty-Two

We returned to our room. I felt flat and Michelle sat on the bed looking worried. "You sure about this?"

I ran my forefinger across my lips and nodded in the direction of the door indicating it was time to exit. We headed for a coffee at the place we ate lunch the day before. This time, I chose a quiet table towards the back. I knew we were being followed. When the waitress came, I asked if anything was happening in the area today. She told me about a street market on Marshalls Row, not too far away, and gave me directions. This might just be what we want to escape from our tail.

"That could suit us."

"Yea. Why don't we need to go out the back door here? They must have a staff exit, emergency exit or something."

"But if we do that, they know we have shaken off their man intentionally. If we lose him at the market, they will just think he's not done his job. Anyway, let's talk about the offer."

"I'm scared Paul. I'm scared you are going to die. I'm scared you don't even know who you are up against or what you are supposed to do. I'm scared that Reeve and Carter don't care if you live or die."

"So, what do I do try and hide without the unknown bad guys finding me or the Special Branch coming after me. That's not going to work for long."

I moved my chair, so I was close to Michelle and put my arm around her.

"This is the best way. I know it's a gamble, but I feel that it just might work, and I'll end up on a beach applying factor 30 to your back without a care in the world."

Michelle was not convinced. I had never seen her so glum. We had only just met but she really cared for me. I suppose we had been through more in a few days than most couples endure during a lifetime. I was in no rush to start playing cat and mouse with our middle aged military man, so I ordered more hot drinks. On the way back from the bathroom I quizzed the waitress on where I could get a couple of phones before returning to the table.

"How much cash have you got?"

"About 150 quid. Thought I might need it."

"Okay. The plan is to lose our tail and head for the store to get phones. If we've lost him, I should be alright going up to the counter and buying them. Was thinking about getting someone to buy them for us – but there's no need is there?' My plan is to get in amongst the market stalls and when I see our man watching from a distance we will dart off and lose him."

We walked out of the coffee house/restaurant, and I saw our man sitting on the same bench opposite, dressed in a blue Harrington Jacket today. I quickly looked away.

"He's there. Try and be as relaxed as possible."

I was firmly entrenched in the moment and my comments brought a smile to Michelle's face.

"Okay Poirot."

Within a few minutes we were at the busy street market. As we entered the market I spoke softly to Michelle.

"When I say go, you follow me. Keep close and don't look around – keep your eyes fixed on my back."

She nods her head, and we walk together at a comfortable pace looking at the stalls. Three quarters of the way down the narrow aisles I stop and inspect some belts on display. Looking to my right, I see our man at the beginning of the market. He looks away as he sees me glancing.

"Go."

Michelle follows me as I go down the side of the stall, turn right and walk back in the direction we came. We get to the end and walk briskly out onto another street. I take a good look around. No signs of our tail.

'Can't see him. You good?"

"I'm good. Got no worries as my man's a top private eye."

I smiled.

"Sarcasm is the lowest form of wit."

We walk another few paces hand in hand, and I spot a local taxi with its distinctive white paint work and aqua bonnet. I wave him down and we quickly jump inside. The bald mature man, who appeared well dressed for a taxi driver, turned to face us.

"Where to, you two?"

"Sainsbury's please."

"Okay but it's not far to walk."

"My man's getting old now. His arthritis is playing up."

We didn't talk any further in the taxi and the driver dropped us off outside the entrance. Michelle paid him. I stood facing her on the pavement and shook my head.

'Getting old? Arthritis? You haven't complained about my fitness until now. You're pushing it a bit now madam.'

Michelle gave me a grin and her face had that look of satisfaction that said, 'I've got one over you'.

"Looks like I've hit a nerve. Definitely need to keep you on your toes."

I shook my head again, smiled knowing I was beaten and marched to the Argos section at the rear of the store. I ordered two burner phones and two SIM cards. Michelle paid cash. We made our way to the men's clothing section which appeared to be the quietest part of the mega store. I fitted the SIM cards and rang Gary.

'Alright Gaz?'

"Not too bad mate – surviving." Look I need you to do something for me straight away. That cash in your account?'

"Good. You will get a text from Michelle in a minute with her account details. Please transfer all the money to her account."

"She's a good friend who I hope to spend the rest of my life with. I'll bring her to meet you soon mate. In the meantime, you alright to do that straight away? Oh, and once you have seen the money depart your account send Michelle a text – just type done." "Good. You'll get the details in a minute or so. Thanks, Gazzer."

I handed the burner to Michelle and read out Gary's number. Within seconds the text was sent. I put my arms around her and kissed her forehead. Michelle put on a convincing Irish accent.

"Do you mind? Conduct yourself we are in a public place."

A genuine smile of happiness spread across her face, not the sarcastic 'told you so' grin I witnessed earlier.

"I bet that took a bit of saying. A good friend who I hope to spend the rest of my life with." I sighed.

"No Michelle. It was easy to say because it's true."

We looked at each other for a couple of seconds, though it seemed much longer. I was content even though a Special Branch detective was tailing us, and an unknown murderer or murderers were on my case. I put my arm around her, and we headed to the exit.

'What now?'

"We head back to our coffee bar or bistro, whatever it is and get some scran. Then we wait until Sherlock finds us. I reckon we head for the beach then. Do you fancy a paddle?"

"This is Brighton, not Marbella. Even if we get lucky and the sea's clean, it is going to be freezing. And I don't fancy seaweed between my toes today either. Not for me. I'll walk on the pebbles with you, and you can immerse yourself in the sea for as long as you like. After you've rolled your shorts up to show the Channel your knees, we can head towards the pier and eat candyfloss."

We strolled through Brighton's busy streets hand in hand. Locals in a rush bumped into us and holidaymakers walked around in loud shirts and T-shirts exposing their milk bottle legs, most of them dawdling without a care in the world. We stopped to look at the odd shop window but did not browse inside any of the shops. In no time we were back at the bistro. Fortunately, a table in the window was available so I could look out for Sherlock. If I am honest, I reckon I was a bit smug following my victory against the man from Special Branch. Surprisingly, Michelle chose not to deflate my ego.

Chapter Forty-Three

I quickly demolished my afternoon tea – I was getting a liking for scones and clotted cream. I had finished before Michelle had reached the halfway mark with her éclair, though she does take the smallest of bites and after each one insists on wiping her mouth whether the fresh cream had dared to infringe her upper lip or not. As I strained the last cup of tea from the pot Sherlock appeared on the bench.

"You enjoy that?"

"It was great. I will be the size of a house if we stay here much longer. You wolfed yours down."

"Okay. Our man's back. He's sitting on the bench. We'll get going in a minute, can you visit the ladies and check to see if Gazzer's text has arrived. We have no way of checking your account with these phones."

I paid the waitress whilst waiting and Michelle nodded on her return letting me know Gazzer had done as promised. We were like two big kids on the beach and at the pier, though neither of us could manage a candyfloss following the large intake of cream. We still had a couple of hours left before dinner.

'Shall we have a snooze by the dome?'

"Snooze. I was only pulling your leg about being an old dodderer. I didn't expect you to turn into one. Go on then –

you will need to be fully recharged when I get hold of you after dinner."

We took the short walk to Pavilion Gardens and hired two deck chairs in the shadows of Brighton Dome. Michelle dug her book out and within 15 minutes I was asleep, later convincing myself I needed the extra rest following my ordeal in hospital.

Chapter Forty-Four

The doctor had arrived early and was waiting when we returned. After a quick check he assured me, I was fine and would have no repercussions. In his opinion there was no need for him to call again. We made our way to the room to shower before dinner. We were both aware that the room was probably bugged or that Special Branch could even be videoing us. We kept our conversations short and bland.

"Okay madam. Are we relaxing indoors or exploring Brighton after dinner?"

'Let's have a stroll along the seafront. Walk off some of those calories we are about to consume.'

Jean did us proud again. Five-star dinner again. She knew I loved old fashioned puddings and had started spoiling me. Tonight, the syrup sponge and custard was a work of art – just like mum used to make. Reeve and Carter came into the dining area about 20 minutes after us and just acknowledged we were there without striking up a conversation. They sat the other end of the room to us out of earshot.

"You ready fatty?"

I smiled and responded.

"Pot, kettle, black."

We thanked Jean and said our goodbyes to Reeve and Carter before exiting from the front door. Walking at a gentle pace we smiled at each other without talking. After a few minutes Michelle broke the silence.

"You okay."

"Yea. I'm good. This is a great break; I'm enjoying it but at the back of my head I just want to get this Special Branch job out of the way, and we can get close to a normal life. Though I am also wondering if I'll end up dead like the other lads."

"You better not end up dead – you have to look after me. Anyway, you're indestructible. Captain Ellis. Super Paul."

We smiled at each other and walked down a quiet street. There were houses ether side, the only folks around were two men chatting around 50 yards away. As we got closer, we noticed they were two ugly bruisers dressed in suits and ties. They had an east of Europe look about them but took no notice of Michelle and me. When we were within ten yards of the pair we heard a car roaring – it was directly behind us. The came to a halt broadside taking up most of the narrow road. It was a gleaming black limousine. The two bruisers rushed towards us grabbing our arms. The driver got out and spoke to us in a strong London accent.

"These two won't be speaking to you."

At that point they both took revolvers out and pointed them at our heads.

"Nether of you will be harmed if you behave yourselves but one wrong move and these boys will blow your heads off. No grey areas with them."

Michelle started breathing quickly as though she was about to start a panic attack.

"Calm down lady. You'll be stopping here whilst your boyfriend is taken to meet someone. He won't be harmed if he's sensible. Within a couple of hours, he should be on his way back to you."

The pair bundled me in the back of the car sitting ether side.

"Don't worry Michelle."

The driver closed the door.

"You run along now – he will be back in no time."

Chapter Forty-Five

The driver pulled away sedately and shouted at me sitting in the back of the car.

"These pair don't speak English Paul, but they will use their guns if they have to. Just do as you're told. I'm taking you to a meeting. You will have a chat with someone very influential and then you can get back to Brighton."

The limousine was out of Brighton within minutes and according to the road signs we were on the way to London. No one talked and the driver put on some mellow music. Though the bruisers were in immaculate black suits and white shirts they gave off a smell that suggested they got ready in a rush this morning and forgot the deodorant. Their body odour would not kill me, but they might. I was thinking about who it was I was being taken to. I could only surmise that it was some big shot and the £10,000 I found was connected to him and he gave the orders to run the bag to London. If that was the case, chances are strong that I will end up dead like the other guys. On 'Death Row' they get a steak and a cigar, I get East Europeans with body odour problems.

We cruised up the M23 and travelled along the M25, which was quiet for once. Under different circumstances, without the sweaty bruisers and the imminent threat of death, the journey would have been good in a limo like this. Whoever owned it did not have to worry about rent for a shabby flat in Kidderminster. I recognised Greenwich as we sped through it on the way to the old Blackwall Tunnel. We were soon surrounded by high rise buildings with glistening glass on the prestigious Canary Wharf. The driver aimed for a building next to the Thames. He parked below and the four of us headed inside after the Londoner had used a key card to get in. I noticed the name of this glitzy high rise, Vanguard Building. I did not see which button was pressed on the elevator, but I guessed it was on the top floor.

Chapter Forty-Six

The two bruisers led me into a hallway and then into a huge open space. The ceiling must have been 30 foot high except where there was a gallery and a semi-spiral staircase leading up to bedrooms I presume. Two huge sofas looked lost in the open space and the tall windows gave a magnificent view of the Thames and London at night. The two henchmen stood next to me, and nothing was said to me for about 90 seconds.

A short balding man in his fifties walked in dressed in a pin stripe suit, shirt and tie looking like a stockbroker. He was accompanied by another bruiser who looked like his personal bodyguard. The small man looked me up and down. but kept his distance choosing not to shake my hand.

"You like what you see Mr Ellis?"

I nodded.

"Not bad for a boy from Czestochowa who attended school with holes in his shoes and went to bed hungry each night. These are some of the trappings of luxury. I'm Wojciech Kaminski. According to reports I am the ninth richest man in the whole world. That is based on legal and declared wealth. In reality, I easily make the top five. Anyhow, that is enough self-publicity from me."

He turned to his right and bellowed.

"Zofia"

"Could you show our guests some hospitality?"

The petite girl had long dark hair and looked no more than 18-years-old. She stood next to Kaminski, like a puppy waiting for a morsel from its owner.

"Mr Ellis. What can we get you to drink?"

I refused his offer, not because I was not thirsty, but I did not fancy the odds on whether or not my drink would be spiked.

Kaminski looked across to the driver.

"Just an orange juice for me," he said.

He didn't bother asking the bruisers.

"You must wonder what is happening? Am I the man who has run your life ragged from the moment you stepped on to that train at Snow Hill station? The answer to that question is yes. You were followed around the UK, attempts made on your life and for what? The item you were given to deliver was a smoke screen. It meant nothing – part of the test to see how you would react.'

"Why were you testing me?"

"I am a very rich man, but no matter how rich you are you do not live forever. I will be gone within six months. I have no children, my body could not make them no matter which specialists I saw, my wives have long since been paid off. I do not want to give them another penny, but I would like to leave my wealth in the right hands, so I found five ordinary Joe's who I thought were hungry and tested them. The winner gets the chance to inherit. You are the winner."

"Why me? I have never run a business."

"Because I did not want some crooked accountant or banker. You had humble beginnings and you have shown you can handle adversity and adapt."

'You said I was one of five – are the others dead?'

Kaminski showed no remorse, human lives were obviously cheap as far as he was concerned.

"They are dead because they lacked your nous. Death beckoned if you failed, but the prize for the winner is astronomical. Billions, not millions at your fingertips."

"If you take the reins, you will have the largest of yachts, homes in Monaco, London and an island in the Caribbean. You can spend freely but I would also expect you to oversee the running of the businesses and continue the good work of my charities."

"This is a lot to digest. I want you to sleep on it. Harry will give you a number to call in the morning so you can give me your answer. If you do not think you can carry out my wishes, I guarantee there will be no repercussions. If you go to the police or our friends at Special Branch, there is nothing you know that can be linked to me. We will speak again tomorrow; I will leave you with Harry.'

Harry led me away and within seconds I heard two gunshots. I turned around to see the bruisers standing over the bodies of Kaminski and his bodyguard, guns in hand.

"Come on."

I followed the driver out to the lift. Once we got inside Harry started talking. He was relaxed you would not think he had just walked out of a room where two men were murdered in cold blood.

"Right son. We will get outside and you're on your own then. You can forget all talk about billions of pounds, but you can walk away with your life and forget this ever happened."

Chapter Forty-Seven

We were back on the street. In the real world as though nothing had happened. Harry took some notes out of his wallet and handed them to me in case I needed a taxi. I stood outside the grandiose Vanguard Building stunned, I was in a state of shock after hearing I had been chased round the country so some old Polish guy could give me billions. After being introduced and hearing his plans for me he was gunned down along with his bodyguard. The billions had gone before they ever arrived, and I was clueless as to what happens next. One thought and one thought only came to my mind. Get out of here fast in case they changed their minds. I would keep to the main roads and find a tube or a Docklands Light Railway station. If I could hail a cab in the meantime, even better. The burner had no maps or internet access so, as regards directions, I was urinating in the wind once more.

A touch of luck came my way as I turned out of the road into Millennium Harbour I saw a sign to Canary Wharf Station – it was just half a mile away. Within 100 yards I got another shock. Reeve and Carter pulled up with a driver. They bundled me into the car and Reeve told me not to say a word. We drove for about a mile and a half. As we got near to Blackwall Tunnel, the driver turned off as he saw a sign to Naval Row car park. The place was desolate. I got scared wondering whether this pair would kill me, and my mind still questioned why they were waiting for me.

Carter spoke sternly.

"Get out of the car."

He went to the boot and returned with a tracksuit and trainers.

"Take everything off including underwear, place your stuff in a pile then put the tracksuit and trainers on, then get back in the car."

Once I was sat in the car in fresh clothes, he emptied the pockets of my trousers. "What's this?" he said holding up the burner.

I thought it best to stay quiet. He took the SIM card out and broke it up before smashing the phone. He put all my clothes, what was left of the phone and my shoes in a pile and set fire to them waiting for them to burn out before we departed. Carter got into the front seat and stayed quiet whilst Reeve questioned me.

"We burnt all your clothes just in case they had placed a bug on you. You can't be too careful."

"So how did you know I was there?"

"We've been watching Kaminski for a while. Two of our guys were outside the apartment block and I'd sent everyone your description when you went missing. One of them called it in when you showed up with a pair of Goons."

I then recalled all events from the time I was kidnapped to when I was left on the street. Carter got on his mobile and told someone to go to Kaminski's apartment as he and his bodyguard had been shot dead. Carter also repeated the descriptions of Harry and the two bruisers that I had given him.

"I want you to relax now. You are safe but might want to lay in tomorrow. That's fine if you do, Jean will make you breakfast anytime you want. We will go over everything with you tomorrow after I have had a chat with my boss."

The chirpy driver parked in front of the former boutique hotel and shouted out. "Home, sweet home."

Not sure whether that is the best of terminology, but I am glad to be back in one piece.

I walked through the hallway and Michelle came running to me flinging her arms round me.

"Oh Paul, I thought I'd seen the last of you."

"You should be so lucky – can't get rid that easy."

She had obviously been crying. her eyes were puffy, and her make-up had run. I did not care how she looked. I was thrilled to see her, the one thing in life that could keep me going regardless of murders, billionaires, and the Special Branch. After looking me up and down, Michelle spent another two minutes just hugging me. Her head was turned to the side, and I suspected her eyes were closed. I dare not guess what she was thinking, I was just grateful she missed me. Jean rustled up some food and we went up to bed. Even though I thought the room was bugged, I told Michelle everything that happened. It was only a repeat of what I told the detectives in the car. I was shattered and told Michelle I had to sleep. She snuggled up to me and as soon as my head touched the pillow, I was asleep.

Chapter Forty-Eight

It turned out I did not need to lie in and was awake at eight. After showering we headed for breakfast. I soon demolished my full English as Michelle delicately picked over her scrambled eggs.

Carter asked me to join him and Reeve at a table in the corner. My request that Michelle joined us was agreed to and Jean bought us pots of coffee and tea with homemade cookies.

"The death of Wojciech Kaminski and his bodyguard will not make it to the newspapers or TV," Reeve announced in a matter-of-fact sort of way. "I have been told that his death on British soil could be embarrassing and as he has no living relatives, we may just get away with it. Kaminski was a private person who refused to have his photo taken or be filmed; hopefully that will go in his favour.

If we had arrested him, we would expect you to have been a witness at his trial, probably from an anonymous location via video. That won't be necessary now. All my boss requires is for us to record all the details, so after breakfast tomorrow you need to repeat everything, you have told us, and we will video it."

"Is that it? All done?"

"More or less. Our problem is we don't know who ordered the hit or hits. The two stooges would probably work for anyone and even if we could find them, they will never tell anyone who employed them. As far as you are concerned that is a problem for us. We don't know who we are up against. Now I don't believe for a minute either of you are in danger and anyone is seeking to knock you off, but my boss is prepared to offer you the same deal we offered, the same anonymity, the same amount of cash over a long period. What do you think?"

"Sounds good."

Carter chipped in: "When we spoke you two had a good idea as to what you wanted to do and where. I want you to spend today talking it over and give me all the details tonight so we can get the wheels in motion."

I looked at Michelle who nodded.

"Sure."

Okay. We won't be hanging around. I'll get everything off to my boss tonight and get an answer back tomorrow. The plan is to get you at your 'start-up' next week.'

Chapter Forty-Nine

Though the place was lovely and had everything we desired. I needed to get out for no apparent reason I felt claustrophobic. The sun shone and Michelle held my hand as we walked through the streets heading for the pier. We walked down the same street where I was abducted, it was very quiet again and no sign of the East European bruisers thankfully. As we got close to the pier, we started discussing our future.

"It's all moving along very quickly now," Michelle commented.

"That's good, isn't it?"

"Yea."

"So, what are we doing?"

"I still like the idea of Crete. We are too young to retire, a bar restaurant gives us work in season. We don't have to work off-season and if we only open evenings, it gives you all day to give me attention and for you to be on my beck and call."

I smiled. I couldn't help it. If another woman had said that I might have walked off. She did mean it. She would expect me to run round after her and treat her like a Princess, but it would be quid pro quo. She would run round for me without asking too and I am sure we would work together well.

We walked down the boardwalk of the pier, it had become chilly, and Michelle snuggled up.

"I like the idea of us two working together. I reckon if we employed a local chef, we could do everything else. Serve food and drinks, clean-up every day and order food and beverages, shop for fresh produce and all that."

"Yea. For a lot of people their dreams become a misery. That's not going to happen to us babe. I have two worries. It is all going very quickly. Why? And the fact that on one hand they do not think you are in danger, but are still prepared to give you the package worries me."

"I'd say there is and could always be a chance of danger, but what do you want to do? Set up in Solihull where we are even easier to find?"

'So, we both agree then, we could be in danger, but are prepared to take the risk."

"Spot on Michelle. We don't have to hide away the rest of our lives, but we won't draw attention to ourselves ether. Anyway, Kaminski has been killed by his own men – if they'd wanted me dead, they would have shot me the same night."

"We know where we want to go. After lunch we will go back and borrow a laptop or visit an Internet Café if we see one."

Chapter Fifty

We sat in the window of our favourite bistro. Waiting for yet more food, I felt relaxed. The sweating, fast heartbeat and constant apprehension appeared to have gone. It had been replaced by excitement. I would not be returning to my dingy flat, or job I was about to be sacked from with little hope for the future. Instead, for the first time in my life, I had found someone who I wanted to be with forever and the added bonus of an easy life where I could walk down to the sea any day I wished. Bit of a change in life, though meeting up with Zorba and Kaminski's heavies was an experience I would not like to repeat in the future.

"You notice something Michelle?"

She shrugged her shoulders.

"No sign of Sherlock. Until now he's followed us every day. But today, no sign of him." "Perhaps he's getting his verruca done."

"Very helpful Michelle. Very helpful. That to me spells out that they thought we were in danger but now Kaminski is sleeping with the fishes, popped his clogs or even kicked the bucket, it appears the boys from Special Branch do not believe our lives are under threat any longer."

"It looks that way, but would you put your life in their hands. From what I see they are a bunch of muppets."

"I don't think they are too much help either, but are we agreed the best option is a bar in the sun."

"Too right – as long as you behave yourself Pauly boy. No wandering off and getting kidnapped. Plus, I have certain standards. You can't let yourself go and become a flabby bartender. You've got to look the part."

I was lost for words. She often had that affect. I just ended up smiling. After eating too much, we made our way across the city centre until we discovered an Internet Café. I paid for an hour and bought a couple of soft drinks. Michelle hogged the keyboard and would not let me near it. I let her get on with it, then ten minutes later she became excited.

"Holey Moley, would you believe it. There's a bar and restaurant for sale in Chofakia." "What-fakia?"

She ignored my childish comment and continued.

"My family rented a great villa about a mile from there. There was two traditional Greek places and two others to eat at. This one, Ramblers, was run by a South African bloke with an older South African woman. It was always busy. They had massive T-bone steaks. Everyone went there for the grill food."

"I'm getting hungry. Sounds great."

"It is not a massive place small bar and a few tables inside, twice as many outside. They didn't open lunchtimes when we were there. The great thing was there were no drunken English, just a few well-behaved plus Swedes Germans, French, and others. They also used to do parties for the Americans at the airbase. No late opening and no hassle. It is what we need – silly money as well, though it is only a small place, not a big resort. We could walk to the beach, it's probably only half a mile away."

I could see she was very excited.

"Okay. Okay. Let's speak to Reeve and Carter later."

Michelle gave me a big beaming smile. It was infectious I was happy because she was happy, though I was not just going along with her – it felt right to me. Crete seemed ideal for a new start in life following the chaos and fear the last few weeks supplied. I paid for another hour on the desktop and got another couple of soft drinks. Michelle showed me the area, the beaches, neighbouring towns, and other restaurants as well as the nearby city, which was about 20 minutes away. Presumably we would need to visit Chania regularly for banks and supplies. It looked nice with a few old buildings and a harbour. We managed to find a few menus online and there were quite a few similarities in produce and prices. It also appeared that none of the tavernas appeared to offer credit card facilities, Michelle confirmed it was all cash when she was there. That's how it works in Greece.

After almost two hours, we saw few challenges for our new business. If we ever felt safe to travel home, there were flights from the airport that was located just 20 minutes away throughout the summer, or via Athens in the winter. For me, I felt like I would never want to return. Would Michelle feel the same about going home? I doubt it. The test would come if any of our parents fell ill. We would not miss the pubs, clubs, and restaurants. I would not miss the shops. I could sacrifice all those things, even a pint of creamy Guinness with the lads, for regular walks on the beach with Michelle. In a couple of weeks, she had become my life, irreplaceable. I pushed those thoughts to the back of my head. You cannot run your life on events that have yet to happen, and we still needed the green light from Reeve and Carter's boss.

"Shall we take a walk across the beach or nip round to the pier?"

"Is that so you can have a nap afterwards. Maybe a deckchair on the pier this time." I smiled and shook my head.

"Greece will suit you, old man. You can have a siesta every afternoon and blame the heat."

"I will have returned to myself by then, completely healed. There will be no stopping me. Let's see how quick you move in the sea."

Chapter Fifty-One

We sat down after dinner with Reeve and Carter. There was no sign of these pair being on holiday. They were still dressed formally as they were when they first rocked up at the hospital. They had the attitude to match their clothes. No light-hearted jokes, down to business immediately. Carter started the dialogue.

"It looks like it is all over bar the shouting. Tomorrow morning, we will record everything on video. There will not be any trials, prosecutions or further investigations of the incident that has happened as the main subject is dead. What we will be doing in the morning is videoing your full account of events, from the moment you were abducted, until we picked you up.

"The boss says he is happy to offer you the same deal we discussed which will be funded by the British taxpayer with no costs borne by you. I do not know where the funds will come from, but it is obviously sanctioned by our department. Do you know what you want to do?"

I looked at Michelle who was sitting next to me, took a long pause and answered.

"Yes. We would still like new identities and the idea of running a bar in Crete suits both of us. In fact, we know of a bar/restaurant in Crete that is available at a low price to buy. We wondered if we could look at the same sort of budget but own the bar/restaurant instead of renting? We will also need a decent size hatchback or estate car and somewhere to live."

Carter smiled and replied.

"We don't get involved in the figures, but if it is the same sort of outlay, I am sure we can sort it. Write down the name of the place and location. We won't mess about. The boss will probably come back to us tomorrow and we will finalise everything then."

Michelle liked what she heard.

"When can we make a move?"

"I should say we can get you out there in four or five-days Michelle. Not sure how long it will take before everything is signed, but there will be somewhere for you to stay whilst it's sorted out."

Chapter Fifty-Two

I felt a lot better in myself but decided it would be best to get out and chat, so we made our way towards the seafront. We were both pleased with our meeting, and I felt everything was moving at 100mph and found it difficult to keep up. But who needs to keep up? I might as well just go with the flow as Michelle was not worried at all. We ended up sitting on a bench watching the tide come in.

"Have you got anything you are worried about Michelle?"

"No. It's great. Probably the best thing that has happened to me. How about you?" "There's two things that I would like to change."

"What's that?"

'Seeing everyone. We won't see our families or friends. Maybe never again. Not sure if we should pay them a flying visit.'

"No. That will make it worse. If things stay cool for a few years we can make plans, then. Can't believe they have still kept this deal open when the bloke's dead. Suppose it's not their money – they don't care. For all we know we won't ever be in danger again. You must forget the family for a while. What else was there?'

"I know we will get new passports and different identities, if it all goes wrong, we might need our old ones."

"I've got mine – it's in my bag."

"What kind of person carries her passport around?"

"I thought I might need it. Got all my cards as well. If we ever need that nine and a half grand, I've got my bank card and passport. As for your passport, I reckon they will be looking out for Paul Ellis and whatever name is on your new one. It doesn't really matter."

"Gazzer's got it anyway. Worst case scenario I get him to send my passport via courier. Is there anything we need to get before we go?"

"We might as well buy anything we need over there. Could do with summer clothes."

"I'll need some shorts and sandals, maybe the odd shirt. I'm going to buy a nice bottle of Scotch on the plane or at the airport."

Chapter Fifty-Three

Our time on the south coast was becoming predictable. Another good evening meal to be followed by a meeting with Reeve and Carter. Though, I felt we were now close to getting what we wanted and with the man behind the deaths now dead himself, I felt safe. Michelle and I sat opposite the Spooks; Carter had a pile of papers in front of him and spoke first.

"Okay you pair, they have really pulled out the stops with this one. We can get you on a plane on Tuesday into Chania. In the short space of 24 hours, we have made a bid on the property, and it has been accepted. The Greeks take their time on anything to do with the law, but we have an agreement that we can pay a low rent from the start of the month up until the day you get the deeds.

"You have been provided with a simple house, not too far away. Again, this will be low rent, but you have the opportunity to change it if you wish. There will be a guy from a car hire company who has his office in the town your restaurant is located meeting you at the airport. You have six-months car hire paid in full and then it's down to you and your allowance. Hopefully the business will be making a profit by then. Any questions?"

"Not at the minute."

"Do you need any of the re-location money now?"

"Don't think so."

"Okay Vicki can supply you with more clothes and you will probably need the odd suitcase or walk on luggage. She will be round after breakfast. Other than that, get yourself ready – you will be picked up at 10am on Tuesday and taken to Gatwick."

Chapter Fifty-Four

It was late afternoon and we sat at a table on the sand by a small café at a cove beach around half-a-mile from our taverna. Michelle was in the process of beating me at chess. We decided on one more soft drink and a last dip in the sea before walking up the hill to start work. We had become part of the café owner's family and often took lunch here and had spent family days with them on Sundays. It had been five months since we'd left England and life could not be better. My relationship with Michelle was perfect. People liked our taverna and the locals were helpful and friendly. Michelle was fluent in Greek, and I was getting there, which helps. We spent every day on the beach, there was a lot of good beaches to choose from. Some days we would be at one beach in the morning and another in the afternoon. We soon forgot about England. After splashing each other in the sea like a pair of teenagers, we made our way up the hill towards the taverna.

"So, madam, is there anything I could do to make life better?"

"Yea get me a Star Bar. No this is even better than I thought, and I was expecting perfection. That blend of work and relaxation is good and we are making a few Euros."

I opened the doors of the taverna. Our chef would be along in ten minutes. He was recommended by a friend, and he had proved to be a great cook, though he has not long graduated in psychology. We gave the place a quick tidy up. Michelle started preparing salad and I sorted the beers and wines. Most important that the punters have a 'cold one' within five minutes of sitting down. Plus, the more they drink the more they spend.

Two old Brits walked in at six o clock. Hours earlier than the rest of our clientele, but I expect that's what time they ate back in Pudsey and refused to change their routine for holiday. It was no problem our chef Thanos who soon had the grill up and running and the couple appreciated the service, leaving a good tip. It was a busy night. Lots of salad starters and mainly steak and Greek pork chops as mains, though we sold the odd fish and traditional Greek dishes plus Prawn Saganaki, a Crete favourite. We were starting to get a few Greeks and Cretans eat at the taverna, which we took as a compliment. The three of us had a quick clean at the end of the night and I decided to call in next morning and spend an hour cleaning up and ordering whatever stock we needed, or even fetching it, before heading to the beach. We sat down, the three musketeers, after another successful battle with the tourists and drank cold beers. Thanos was exhausted and sweating heavily, though he refused the offer of another Mythos. I gave him his share of the tips and he trudged over to his scooter to ride home for a well deserved rest.

Michelle came over and sat on my lap.

"Another good night Rodders. This time next year we'll be mill-ya-nairs." We kissed for what seemed like a long time. Neither of us wanted to part lips. I looked up and said: "Life is the best it's ever been."

"You better believe it."

Chapter Fifty-Five

Our place was less than a mile from the taverna. We spent little time there, but it was cosy, and it was ours. Michelle drove and dropped me off just after ten and she headed to the supermarket. I washed all the glasses and started drying them with a tea towel before stacking them behind the bar. CNN played on the TV above the bar. I would have preferred a British newsreader telling me about excessive rain in Wales and the shortage of nurse and teachers, but I made do with the American news channel.

"One of the world's richest men died yesterday. Wojciech Kaminski..."

I dropped a glass but did not look at the floor. My eyes were firmly fixed on the TV and the ticker that rolled at the bottom of the screen confirmed Kaminski's death.

"... suffered a heart attack and died within minutes at one of his residences in Florida last night. The Polish raised billionaire entrepreneur was reported to be the globes ninth richest man with interests in steel, agriculture, and property. He was something of a philanthropist, spending millions ensuring many countries in Africa now have a continuous supply of water. His charities have also prevented thousands of Polish men, women, and children from living in poverty. He was a very secretive man, not allowing images to be taken of him.

One of his relatives have supplied AP with this picture taken in the last 18-months."

The photograph came on to the screen. It was nothing like the man I met.

"Our thoughts go out to Mr Kaminski's family."

The coverage switches to a female presenter.

"Fires in California raged..."

I was dumbstruck. I walked over to the shelves behind the bar and took down a bottle of Johnnie Walker blue label Scotch whiskey that I had been saving for a special occasion or rainy day whichever might be more appropriate. The dust from the top of the bottle was quickly wiped down, before I cracked it open and poured myself a very large measure. It went down easy, though I cannot say I appreciated the quality, I just needed a large dose of alcohol.

Why did they use a man who pretended to be Kaminski? They must have known the truth would come out when he died. The two Special Branch men must be involved, is British intelligence behind the plot? If it was, why did they not just kill me like the others instead of setting Michelle and me up for life? It is mad. If that was not Kaminski that was shot, who was it? Did they kill those two or was it a show for me – why would they need to do that?

I sat on a bar stool and watched the news, though I could not tell a soul what I had been watching. My head was elsewhere. Two more glasses of Scotch were soon emptied.

Chapter Fifty-Six

Within half-hour of learning about Kaminski's death. I had a visitor – someone I had not seen for five months. It was Carter, still dressed in formal clothes. He must have stood out on a plane full of guys in Hawaiian shirts and khaki shorts.

"You don't look pleased to see me. What's with all the broken glass?"

Carter looked up at the TV.

"You been watching the news? Interesting stuff, isn't it?"

"What's all this about? Who died at Canary Wharf? Did they die and why were you bothered with me? Is the government behind all this?"

Carter took a gun out and pointed it casually at me with his elbow bent.

"You've got no need to worry about answers to those questions. I can say that Reeve and I might have been working freelance, but I'm not going to bother letting you know all the details because you won't around for much longer. You could say you have served your purpose."

Where I stood in the corner of the bar, tucked away was a baseball bat. I had never had to use it – we inherited it with the property. I was trying very hard not to look at it.

"So, where's Michelle?"

"Shopping."

"That's a shame. I'd have loved to have seen your gorgeous Brummie bird. Another time maybe. Anyway, before I go let's have a drink for old times' sake."

I passed Carter a glass. He put his gun down on the counter ready to pour two glasses. Now was my chance. I picked up the baseball bat with both hands and struck him across the cheek with all my might. He stumbled to one side before falling backwards and there was an ugly thud as his head hit the stone floor. I ran round the counter. Carter was motionless. I checked his wrist for a pulse and then his neck. Nothing. He had left a small amount of blood on the floor, but that was it. Carter was dead and it was me who had killed him.

I did not shake; I was quite relaxed and walked to the counter and poured another large Johnnie Walker Blue. I had just killed someone in cold blood, yet that did not trouble me. I was worried that I was not worried – what kind of bloke had I become? The one thing that did keep running through my head was the hard, cold fact that I would be on the run now – possibly forever. If Michelle could not hack it, I knew I could not do it on my own. Five months of paradise followed by the rest of my life on the run – just your luck Paulie boy. When I was on the run before it was frightening. Now I know different characters are involved and maybe even the British government, but who are these people and why me? I am no wiser – I don't even know who the enemy is.

ACKNOWLEDGEMENTS

It is great to have an idea for a book or a film but finishing the product needs more than hard work. Support and encouragement are essential to keep the author focused.

I have been fortunate that Bex has been Captain Sensible and was always there when I needed her. Nel has this great knack of being able to say the right things at the right times. She is never wrong! Katherine has read every word I have wrote and has this great ability to know where a story should be heading and tell me in the nicest of ways. My brother Peter has been the one constant throughout my writing career forever encouraging and offering new ideas.

A big thank you must be given to the lecturers on the Creative Writing course at the University of Wolverhampton. Tired old eyes were refocused and inspired thanks to them and I endorse the saying 'you are never too old to learn'.

ABOUT THE AUTHOR

The author was born in 'The Black Country', west of Birmingham, England and now resides further west in South Shropshire. After spending 20 years as a journalist, PN Campion decided it was time to move in a new direction. He signed up for Creative Writing at the University of Wolverhampton, which re-ignited his love for writing.

Cashing Out is the first novel from PN Campion and two other books are on the anvil, one of which is a sequel to *Cashing Out*. The former journalist intends to keep writing books as well as promoting three film scripts he recently wrote.

Thanks for reading Cashing Out.

If you have enjoyed it, please do consider writing a brief review on the platform you acquired this book, to help other readers find it too.

Contact: info@baveneypress.com

Ingram Content Group UK Ltd.
Milton Keynes UK
UKHW040619170523
421882UK00004B/65

9 798215 653326